My Kingdom for a Sorceress

MW00911054

Laura Josephsen

Text copyright © 2017 by Laura Josephsen
All rights reserved.

ISBN-13: 978-1975752927
ISBN-10: 1975752929

This book is a work of fiction. Names, characters, places, and events are either products of the author's imagination or are used fictitiously.

Cover image from pixabay.com.

For my husband, Ryke,
For all the adventures we've had,
All the dragons we've fought,
And all the battles we've won.
With you, I'm home.

1 – Arrow

Wen stood outside the dragon's cave, his shield on one arm and a small glass bottle of invincibility potion clutched in his fist. He looked up at the full moon shining brightly down on him, trying to judge if it was in the right position. The contents of the glass bottle were starting to glow, so he supposed it probably was.

Mindful of the instructions the witch had given him, he uncorked the lid with his teeth, turned the bottle three times clockwise, once counterclockwise, and downed it in three swallows while jumping up and down on his right leg. Nothing happened, and he had a brief moment of panic that he had missed a step.

No, no, he was positive he had done everything correctly.

Wen's skin began to glow ever so faintly, and he let out a soft, "Ha!" as he pocketed the bottle and cork. He drew his sword with a quiet *schnick* of metal on scabbard, cleared his throat, and called, "Come forth, you monst—"

Someone darted past him in clothes that clanged and clattered. Wen's mouth snapped shut as a tiny knight ran straight toward the cave. Where the blazes had he come from?

The knight wore only half a suit of armor—maybe less than half. He had a breastplate and a helmet; his legs were covered in loose trousers and long boots. A wide sheath hung from his belt and he held a short club aloft.

As the knight disappeared into the cave, Wen hastily

1

ran forward, shouting, "Hey! *Hey!* That's my dragon!"

A burst of flame poured from the cave. The knight dove out of it, somersaulted forward, and jumped to his feet. An earth-shattering roar and another burst of flame were followed by tremendously thudding footsteps as the dragon emerged. Its scales were a bright, poisonous blue. Its head, face, and tail were rimmed with sharp spikes at least as long as Wen's arm. It was much, much bigger than Wen had expected. How had it even managed to fit inside the cave?

Wen glanced at his faintly glowing skin, took a deep breath, and moved forward with his sword and shield held at the ready. The knight danced in front of the dragon. Wen winced as the dragon's head snapped forward. He half expected the knight to get swallowed in one or two chomps, but somehow, the knight ended up on the dragon's snout, clutching a spike and still holding his club.

Wen almost missed seeing the tail swinging toward him. He threw himself to the ground and the deadly tail whipped past his head so closely it skimmed his hair. It wouldn't have killed him, not with the potion he'd drunk, but it could have knocked him a good distance away.

Wen got to his feet and shouted at the knight, "You idiot, what are you *doing?* You're going to get yourself killed!" Wen dodged a claw aimed his way and ducked the tail again. The dragon's head rounded on him. The knight still clung to its snout, trying to hit it in the eye with his club, but his arm was too short to reach.

"Back off!" The high voice calling from inside the helmet sounded tinny through the metal. "I got here first!"

A great well of indignation rose up inside of Wen. "You did n—" A burst of fire from the dragon hit him full-blast. It was warm on his skin, almost unpleasantly so, but he was alive, with his skin still glowing cheerily.

His skin. *All* of his skin. The witch whom he'd bought the invincibility potion from had told him he would be completely safe for ten minutes, unharmed by claws or fire or teeth crunching or even drowning. (He hadn't been sure how drowning in a dragon was relevant, unless the witch thought the dragon could swallow him whole and he'd drown in the stomach acid before he burned in it.)

2

The witch hadn't mentioned that his clothes wouldn't be safe. He was so dismayed to see them completely burned off, leaving only ashy trails on his skin, that he missed the warning shout from the knight. The dragon's foot swiped him and hit his shield hard enough to send him sailing into the trees surrounding the cave. He slammed into a trunk, but it didn't hurt. No broken bones, no fatal crunching. He hit the ground with his shield pinned awkwardly beneath him.

How was he supposed to slay a dragon while he was naked!? It would have been embarrassing even if there hadn't been someone else there to watch!

There was a shout, and the knight was thrown off of the dragon and flung through the air. He crashed down right on top of Wen, who, thanks to the potion, wasn't even winded. He was just very, very mortified.

The knight scrambled off of him and turned his helmeted head down toward Wen. "Ahh! Where are your clothes!?"

"They were burned off, what does it *look like*?"

"Well, put something on!"

The dragon pounded toward them, the *stomp, stomp, stomp* of its feet quaking the ground.

"I'd love to, but unless you think I have time to sew some leaves together, I'm kind of out of luck!" Wen jumped up and covered himself with his shield, which now had a dent in it. The knight was tinier than he'd thought; the top of his helmet only came halfway up Wen's chest.

The knight seized Wen's arm and yanked him behind a large tree. Small or not, he was strong. Flames blazed past them and numerous trees around them caught fire.

"Sit still," the knight shouted. "I'll get you some clothes." He pointed his club at Wen, and a moment later, a faint light shot out of the club and spread over Wen's body. Magic? A magic club? Well, that wasn't as weird as the magic tobacco pipe he'd once come across someone using.

A tingling sensation swept over Wen's body. The dragon roared and more fire blasted past them. If they didn't move soon, they were going to have burning branches dropping around them.

Wen had more pressing matters, though. Whatever the knight had done, the glow of the magic invincibility had

3

suddenly disappeared from his skin—which was now a very lovely shade of green.

"Oh, oops!" the knight said. "Wait, I can fix that."

Before Wen could protest, the club was pointed at his face. The lower half of his body was suddenly covered, not with clothes, but with a bright purple, fluffy towel. His skin was still green and not glowing.

Another roar from the dragon, and a tree smashed down beside them, sending sparks of fire and blazing branches raining down. Wen ducked and covered his head with his hands.

"There, that'll do in a pinch. Now excuse me; I've got to take care of this dragon." The knight leapt nimbly around the burning foliage and back toward the dragon.

Disbelieving, angry, and now worried because he wasn't sure his invincibility was working, Wen stood and picked his way out of the fiery area, clutching the towel around his waist and trying to keep his grip on his sword and shield. He stepped on a rock with his bare foot and pain shot up his leg.

Half a dozen curses exploded out of him. His invincibility *was* gone, and the dragon was thrashing about and breathing fire through the trees while the little knight darted around it with his club.

Wen gritted his teeth in determination. He paused to tuck the towel more firmly in place, hefted his shield up, clutched his sword, and strode toward the dragon. It was stupid, very, very stupid, to approach the dragon without magical protection, but if the knight could distract it enough that Wen could just get to the dragon's vulnerable underbelly, he might stand a chance. He *had* to try; it had taken him a month just to get this far.

Light flashed out of the knight's club, and suddenly the dragon had a wreath of enormous flowers about its neck. Another flash of light, and a pile of rocks fell out of nowhere and landed on the dragon's head.

The rocks didn't deter the dragon at all. It shook them off, whirled around, and tried to slam the knight with its tail. The knight jumped and launched himself onto the dragon's tail in between the spikes. As the knight clambered up along the sharp ridge on the dragon's back, Wen ran

4

forward, eyeing the fleshy, exposed underbelly while the dragon tried to bite the knight off its back. The knight held his club up. The light flashed and Wen couldn't tell what it had done—until he saw a cat leaping off of the dragon's back and streaking away into the darkness. Two more cats followed, and Wen didn't let the thought that the sorcerer knight had conjured cats sidetrack him. He was close to the dragon—so close that he could truly appreciate how long and sharp the claws looked, claws that could rip through him in an instant.

One giant eye fixed on him. The dragon's head swiveled toward him completely, teeth bared, and Wen did the only thing he could think of: He whipped off his towel and flung it across the dragon's face, covering one of its eyes. He rolled on the ground to avoid the teeth, and in the moment when the dragon was busy shaking the towel off its face, Wen somersaulted underneath it and jammed the sword up into its belly. It took all of his strength to push it in and then drag it along the dragon's fleshy underside. Sticky blood and fluids poured down on him, and the dragon howled in pain.

Wen barely rolled out from under the massive dragon before it came crashing down—thankfully, not on top of him, but it was close. He held his shield against his body, taking deep, heaving breaths. One of the dragon's claws was centimeters from him, and it jerked with the death throes of the monster. Wen scrambled backward, and only when the dragon stopped moving did he heave a sigh of great relief and flop backward on the ground. The shield covered his privates and his sword was beside him. The acrid smell of smoke stung his nostrils as the fire in the forest raged behind him.

"You!" The glow of the moon above him was obstructed when the tiny knight stood over him, hands planted on hips. "You slew my dragon!"

"Your dragon?" Wen sat up, careful to clutch his shield close. "In case you hadn't noticed, all of the nearby towns are under the most widespread sleeping enchantment I've ever seen. It took me a month to trace the cause of the spell and plan a way to end it. A month! Whose twisted idea was it to tie a sleeping spell to a dragon's life, I ask you?"

"Exactly!" the knight said furiously. "Do you know how rare that is? Do you know what it would have meant if I could have taken the enchantment off it? But, no, you great big lark, you had to come in with your sword swinging and *slay it!*"

"You're the one who came barging in out of nowhere and took away my invincibility spell. It cost me a fortune! *And you made my skin green!*" Wen held up his arms and shook them at the knight.

The knight stomped his foot. "I can fix that!"

Wen scrambled back, dragging the shield with him. "No, thank you. I've seen how you fix things."

"Now you're insulting my magic! Just stay still!" The knight pointed his club at Wen, who cringed but had nowhere to go as the light from the club hit him. His skin prickled and then itched like mad, no doubt due to the pink feathers he'd sprouted everywhere.

"Ahhhh! I look like a pink chicken!"

"I think you look absolutely fetching."

"If you—"

"Oh, get a grip. One more time."

Wen squeezed his eyes shut as the light flowed over him. The itching disappeared, and he cautiously peeked one eye open, fearing that maybe he'd sprouted extra fingers or grown horns. But his skin was back to its normal shade, he had the proper number of digits, and when he felt around his head, all he touched was his hair—no horns or anything else unusual. He tugged a lock of hair forward and peered up at it, relaxing a little more when he saw that it was still brown.

"Quick, what color are my eyes?" he asked.

The helmet leaned toward him. "Green. They're supposed to be, aren't they? I've never changed someone's eye color before, but maybe with your skin being green—"

"No, no, they're supposed to be green," Wen said hastily. He spotted the fluffy, purple towel nearby and scooted toward it. He grabbed it and slipped it under the shield, tucking it all around himself.

The knight plopped down in front of him. "Now what am I supposed to do?"

"Go find someone else to practice magic on."

6

The knight kicked at the ground, whether in anger or frustration or something else, Wen didn't know and really didn't care. He was sticky and smelly and mostly naked. All he wanted to do was clean his sword, clean himself, and sleep. He could take care of the aftermath of the broken enchantment when he didn't smell like dragon innards.

"You wouldn't have been able to kill that thing without me," the knight said. "I distracted it."

"I wouldn't have needed you to distract it if you hadn't taken away my invincibility."

Wen had a feeling the knight was glaring at him under the helmet. "I could have broken the enchantment without killing it, you know," the knight said. "Probably. Maybe. It depends on what kind of magic it was."

"Great, and then what?" Wen asked. "The villages would be terrorized by it once they woke up from their magic sleep. Killing it took away the enchantment *and* sspared all the locals the trouble of dealing with the dragon."

The knight tried to rub his face and was thwarted by his helmet. He made a frustrated noise and pulled the helmet off.

Wen stared. His mental image of a tiny man with a high voice melted away. All right, then. A girl. Pale, pale red hair—so light it was almost blonde in the moonlight—spilled around her shoulders. A pair of blue eyes peered out at him from underneath wispy bangs and her mouth was pursed as she scowled ferociously.

She would have done better to keep her helmet on if she wanted him to take her seriously—her button nose, smattering of freckles, and delicate features were too adorable to make her look scary at all.

"What are you, twelve? What are you doing out here by yourself?" Wen asked incredulously.

She glowered more darkly. "I'm *sixteen*, thank you." His age. She sure didn't look it. She set her helmet on her lap and tousled her sweaty hair. "What's your name? Or should I just walk around calling you Dragon Slayer Who Stole My Chance of Breaking a Powerful Enchantment?"

Wen tried to muster as much dignity as he could while wearing a bright purple towel and realizing that a girl had seen him completely naked. "Wen."

"What do you mean, *when*? I want to know now, obviously, or I wouldn't have asked."

"No, *Wen*. My name is Wen. It's short for Wenceslas."

"Wenselas."

"No, Wen-ces-las," he said slowly.

"Wen-le-sus."

"Wen. Ces. Las."

"Wind is lost."

"WENCESLAS!"

"When's the sauce!"

He was close to throttling her. He really was. Then he saw the way she was smirking wickedly at him.

"Wenceslas, all right," she said. "You can call me Arrow."

"I can call you Arrow?" Wen raised a brow. "That's not your name?"

"Arrow's what I go by."

She had given him such a hard time with his name that he felt it only fair he poke back. "Why Arrow? You carry a club."

"Club has a very harsh sound to it. Arrow's all nice and smooth and flowing." She waved her club through the air. Wen tensed, half afraid it would shoot some crazy magic at him, but no light came out of it.

"Can you use a bow and arrows?" Wen asked.

"Nope, sure can't! I don't need to. I have magic."

"Right." Wen drew out the word. "Magic that can turn a person green and conjure a towel, a wreath of flowers, a pile of rocks, and some cats."

Arrow's face turned the color of her hair, and her lips pursed into that very not scary, furious pout. Wen looked at her with mild amusement. "Can you do magic?" she demanded.

"No."

"Then who are you to talk?" Arrow picked up her helmet and stood, stretching her arms in front of her. She faced the trees still burning behind them and held her club high, swinging it in a wide circle. A gust of wind nearly blew Wen over, and Arrow tilted sideways. If she hadn't been wearing a breastplate, Wen thought she might have been blown away.

Arrow paused, then swung the club again. Small chunks

of ice fell out of the sky. One clonked Wen on the head, but before he could raise his shield for protection, Arrow swung a third time, and what must have been the equivalent of a pond of warm water dropped on top of them. The best thing Wen could say about it was that it washed most of the dragon slime off him, and he didn't smell quite as smoky. He pushed his soaking hair out of his eyes. The fire in the forest had been extinguished, and Arrow did a weird, happy little dance in the moonlight, her breastplate glinting with water droplets.

Looking quite pleased with herself, she sank back down in front of Wen. "So, Wenceslas, why did you spend a month uncovering this enchantment? I think I deserve to know, since you took this chance away from me. Oh, wait. Let me guess. You're after a reward? No, you don't look much like the reward type. You're a hero! You've got the sword and everything! You just can't resist going from place to place rescuing the needy and despondent. You—"

He cut her off before her imagination could lead her too far astray. "I'm a prince."

2 – The Giftcurse

Arrow immediately made a face. "A prince? Ugh! I should have known. Let me guess. Third son? Everyone knows the third son's supposed to do all those hero quests and be all fantastic." Her face was still scrunched in dislike. "Are you on a quest to rescue your foolish elder brothers who ignored every magical instruction they were given? Are you looking for a cure for your ill father?"

"Not a third son," Wen said glumly. "Worse." He gazed morosely at the nearby dragon corpse. "Seventh son of a seventh son."

"Oh, double ugh! I'm so sorry." Arrow really did look sympathetic. "That's an awful lot of pressure on you, isn't it? But...are you sure you don't know magic? Do you have anything magical? The last two seventh sons I met had some awfully powerful magic. One of them had a penchant for turning people into glass when he breathed on them. Thought it was quite funny."

"I told you, I can't do magic. Believe me, my parents did a lot of tests and stuff to make sure."

Arrow leaned close, her freckled nose centimeters from him and her bright eyes peering into his, as if she could find some hidden magic inside him if she got close enough. Wen clenched his shield tighter over his towel.

"No magic," Arrow said quietly, "but...magicked?" Her face got even closer. Wen's eyes crossed trying to focus on her. "You *are* magicked, aren't you? With something really, really strong." She leaned back and pointed her club at him.

He ducked. "Stop pointing that thing at me!"

"I'm just going to do a simple diagnostic spell. Don't

10

worry. I'm good at those. I only made someone sprout a turtle on their nose *once.*"

Wen grabbed Arrow's arm and pushed it so the club wasn't aimed at him. "How about I just tell you?"

She lowered her club. "Oh, well, I guess that works too."

"Not here. I really need to get some proper clothes. I think I saw an inn at the nearest town. They should all be awake now."

"All right, but you might as well tell me about your enchantment while we walk. Unless you have a horse or something around here?"

"I left Bay tied in the town and came on foot," Wen explained. "I didn't really want the dragon to eat him." He picked up his sword and wiped it as best he could on the wet towel still wrapped around him. His sheath had been burned away, so he held the sword and picked his way awkwardly into the forest with Arrow at his side. The ground sloped downward toward the nearest town.

"Hang on, I'll give us some light." Arrow waved her club in a small circle, and a stream of bubbles shot from the end of it. She made a "tch" noise and waved it again, and a bright glow surrounded the end of the club like a torch. "Let me just grab my stuff." She ran over to a section of trees on the opposite side of the clearing and returned with a large bag slung across her back. With the helmet in one hand and the club in the other, she skipped over the blackened branches and ashes into the unburned part of the forest.

Moving was much more difficult for Wen. He had to walk carefully over rocks and twigs while being weighed down by his sopping towel.

"So, Wenceslas, tell me about this magic on you." Arrow leapt on top of a fallen, dead tree and did a neat front flip to land on the other side. Wen blinked twice. He couldn't even do that empty-handed, and Arrow was holding a club, helmet, and a bag. He climbed over the fallen tree and jumped when something streaked past him with a yowl.

It was just one of the cats, undoubtedly terrified because Arrow had brought it from whatever happy place it had been in and dropped it on top of a dragon.

"It started at the celebration for my birth," Wen began. "Dad had a bit of magic, being the seventh son, but everyone

11

was sure I'd be a pillar of greatness or some such. They invited some of the local fairy godmothers, the same ones who had always been invited to my brothers' celebrations."

"Oh!" Arrow said with understanding. "It's fairy godmother magic on you!"

"Yes. It was pretty standard at first. One fairy godmother wished good health on me—worked, too, I've never had so much as a cold my whole life. Another wished a lovely singing voice on me. Not sure what good she thought that'd do, but Mum was quite pleased. The third fairy godmother—well, I guess she arrived rather tipsy; she said something to my parents about some goblin wedding party—and then, quick as you please, gave me *her* blessing."

Arrow paused on top of a stump and fixed wide eyes on him. "You were magicked by a drunken fairy godmother?"

"Yes. Before Mum and Dad could stop her or ask her to sober up first or anything, she said, 'Wenceslas shall be a great hero. He shall rescue a princess from her enchantment and marry her by his seventeenth birthday'—I hear she was kind of a romantic—'and failing this, he shall prick his finger on a glass coffin and he shall die.' I guess she was awfully embarrassed when she'd sobered up and heard she'd cursed me to die when she meant to bless me, but it was too late."

Arrow nodded. "Once fairy godmother magic is cast, it's impossible to remove. Even the fairy godmother who cast it can't remove it, but they can alter it slightly. Please tell me she added an addendum to her drunken spell."

"She did. She said I wouldn't die if I pricked my finger on a glass coffin; I'd fall into an eternal, enchanted sleep and only true love's kiss would wake me."

"That," Arrow said definitively, "is the most *backward* gift I have ever heard, and I've heard a lot. Most people prick their fingers on spinning wheels. How would you prick it on a glass coffin, unless the coffin was broken? Who would even make a coffin out of glass?"

"You'd be surprised." Wen bit his cheek as he stepped on a sharp stick. "I came across a princess in an enchanted sleep in a glass coffin once; she'd been living in a forest with seven dwarves."

"And your fairy godmother put a true love's kiss addendum on a *prince*?" Arrow shook her head. "I'll bet you were

12

teased a lot for that."

"You have no idea. Six older brothers, remember? Between the whole true love's kiss addendum and being an unmagical seventh son of a seventh son, I had quite an interesting childhood."

"So you're out here trying to rescue a princess?" Arrow asked.

Wen nodded. "The local princess fell under the sleeping enchantment in one of the towns here."

"Why bother hunting for princesses? I'd take my chances with the enchanted sleep instead of searching for someone to marry." Arrow wrinkled her nose. "Unless the spell compelled you to go out hunting for them. Fairy godmother gifts are tricky."

"That's exactly it," Wen said. "Pretty much the moment I hit puberty, I just *couldn't* sit still at the castle. It was like the magic on me was trying to prod me into fulfilling my gift. Curse. Giftcurse. There needs to be a word for that."

"Giftcurse completely works," Arrow said. "I'm stealing that from now on. So, Wenceslas, how did this giftcurse force you out of your castle? You do live in a castle, don't you, not a floating city or a kingdom under the ocean?"

"Just a normal, stone-and-mortar castle. Most interesting thing about it is the flying crocodiles in the moat. They're a dreadful nuisance and they breed like mad. Anyway, if I tried to stay there too long, all sorts of things would start happening. Sometimes I felt like there were bugs crawling all over in my bedsheets. Sometimes there was this faint screaming in my ears until I left. Stuff like that. As long as I was wandering around looking for a princess to rescue, I was all right. But my task is nearly impossible. It's getting harder and harder to find enchanted princesses. There are so many princes and third sons going on quests. And it's become quite popular for some kings and queens to willingly enter their daughters into a prick-a-finger-on-the-spinning-wheel spell agreement with a neighboring kingdom."

"Oh, yes, I've heard all about that," Arrow said. "They already have the prince picked out and everything—they just want to make sure he's worthy of their daughter or some such nonsense."

"I've yet to come across an enchanted princess who wasn't waiting for someone else. I've managed to bring several of them out of their spells, but they didn't want to marry me," Wen said. "I was kind of relieved, honestly. I really don't want to get married yet, but I have to keep trying or the giftcurse makes me crazy. At this point, it's either marriage or sleep until my true love can kiss me. I haven't *got* a true love, so there's a good chance I might sleep forever."

"Maybe," Arrow said, "but you might be all right. Some girl might lay eyes on you and get all fluttery and convince herself she's your true love. Although I've heard about plenty of true love enchantments never breaking, so I guess it's a risk either way."

"Honestly, I just want it to be over with so I can stop wandering all over the place."

"How long until you turn seventeen?"

Wen sighed. "Twenty-two days."

"Well, surely you wouldn't be stupid enough to go near a glass coffin after your seventeenth birthday, but fairy godmother enchantments have a way of coming true on their own," Arrow said. "I knew one girl who was cursed to eat a poisoned apple, and she was pretty smart—paranoid of eating fruit altogether. Didn't even drink juice. But one day a tiny sliver of poisoned apple ended up inside her supper—no idea how it got there."

"I know; I've seen some of the things that have happened even when people are careful," Wen said. "You just don't mess with fairy godmother magic." He paused, a sudden thought occurring to him. "I don't suppose you're an enchanted princess?"

Arrow snorted. "Ha! No."

"Ah, well. It was worth asking."

They stumbled—or rather, Arrow leapt and Wen stumbled—through the edge of the trees. Spread out before them was one of the three towns that had been under the sleeping spell. The air now echoed with loud voices calling to each other, and torches dotted the road and shone from cottage windows.

Arrow jumped up and down at the edge of the forest, waving her club and her helmet and yelling, "Hello, you beautiful villagers!" as loudly as she could. "Come on!" She bounded toward the town as several people moved into sight, silhouetted against all the torchlight.

Wen followed on Arrow's heels, but she was much faster than he was in his towel, and by the time he'd reached her, a small group had gathered around her. She was waving back at Wen and explaining about how they had tackled the dragon together. She seemed to have forgiven him for stealing her chance to break the sleeping enchantment.

"—and then he threw his towel on its face and got under it to stab it," Arrow was saying. "And your sleeping spell was broken."

The villagers cheered, and one woman called, "Three cheers for the naked hero!"

Heat flushed Wen's cheeks and he glared at Arrow, who only bounced on her toes and winked at him. "I'm Arrow," she declared. "This is Winces Lots."

"Three cheers for Winces Lots!"

***

Wen was quickly provided with some faded clothes that smelled old and faintly like mildew and an ancient scabbard for his sword, and the villagers poked around for usable food supplies. They were hungry, and their animals were hungry, and after two years in an enchanted sleep, there wasn't a whole lot of food lying around.

"There's a *ton* of dragon meat!" Arrow called into the chattering crowd. "Just through the forest up at the cave. It's all yours. You should be able to get a good price on the dragon parts, too." She waved exuberantly and fell into step beside Wen as he headed back to his chestnut gelding, Bay, tied to a dilapidated post outside an equally dilapidated inn. "You know," she continued, "whoever cast this sleeping spell did a bang-up job with tying it to a dragon, but not so great with the area's upkeep."

"Maybe they didn't care if the towns fell into disrepair."

"Mm. Oh, is this your horse? Hello, you sweet, gorgeous thing!" Arrow dropped her club and helmet and plastered herself to Bay's flank, winding her fingers through his mane with one hand and rubbing his nose with the other.

Bay made a half-huff, half-whinnying noise, and his large brown eyes fixed on Wen as if to ask what in the world was happening. Wen shrugged and said, "Bay, Arrow. Arrow, Bay."

"You are *so* lovely," Arrow said. "Yes, you are a lovely horse, aren't you?"

Bay's whicker sounded very agreeing, and he nudged Arrow with his nose. Wen walked past her and untied Bay from the post. "Good job waiting here, Bay," he said in a low voice as he gave the horse a pat. He wasn't sure Bay heard him over Arrow's crooning.

Bay snuffled first into Wen's right shoulder, then his left.

"I'm fine, really," Wen assured.

Bay huffed and snorted.

"Yes, I know I smell like dragon and smoke. And mildew now, too. But I'm fine." Wen unfastened one of his saddle-bags and offered Bay a handful of oats before taking a long drink of water from his canteen.

"I had a horse once," Arrow said wistfully. "Hollinberry. My father decided I was spending more time with him than with my studies and if I was going to be a proper sorceress, I should learn to fly on broomsticks or make seven-league boots or at least give Hollinberry wings."

"Did you?" Wen offered his canteen to Arrow.

She only stepped back from Bay to take the canteen. "Thank you." She gulped down a lot of water and then answered, "The broomstick was a disaster. It hated me. If I could convince it to fly, it would try to throw me off as soon as I gained any height at all. The seven-league boots were more like seven-meter boots. My brothers laughed so hard. Oooh, it made me so angry, I put a tickling spell on them till Mother found me out and made me take it off. Then I sort of turned one of them into a chipmunk trying to take the tickling spell off." She handed him his nearly empty canteen. "And I couldn't bear to give Hollinberry wings. He loved running so much and he was so beautiful as he was. I didn't see why he had to change for my sake. So Father sold him to some desert nomads."

"If you don't have a horse, how did you get here?"

"I got a ride on a flying carpet for the first part of the

journey, but the driver insisted on going to some fancy-schmancy ball at this palace, so I borrowed a carriage from a princess in a huge hurry. I gave her some gold and everything, but she neglected to tell me the stupid thing would turn into a watermelon at midnight! Then I conjured a pig and rode it for a while, but it abandoned me, so I walked the rest of the way. I just thought if I could dis-enchant this dragon..." She scuffed the ground with her toe. Then she rolled her shoulders, as if throwing off her gloom, and said, "So, what next?"

"What's next for *me* is getting a few hours of sleep at a nice little pond I passed a while back and going to visit the local castle tomorrow."

Arrow made a face. "To see if the princess wants to marry you? What if she doesn't?"

"Then I look for the next enchanted princess." Three more weeks. Only three more weeks, and one way or another, this would be finished.

Wen swung himself up onto the saddle. He chose his words carefully. "It was *enchanting* to meet you. I wish you success in your—"

"Wait, wait!" Arrow leapt in front of Bay and waved her arms wildly. "I'll come with you!"

"Come with me?" Wen apprehensively eyed Arrow's club as she scooped it up off the ground. She tucked it into the large leather sheath strapped to her belt and shoved her helmet on her head, pushing the visor up so he could see her face.

"Look, if you marry Princess Snooze-A-Lot, I'll leave you to wedded bliss"—she grimaced—"and be on my way. If you *don't* marry her, you'll be off looking for more enchantments, right?"

Wen thought he saw where she was going with this. "Enchantments *I* have to break to fulfill my giftcurse," he pointed out. "I can't have a sorceress break them for me."

"That's fine. I don't need to break them, but it would be good to study them—and you never know what magic you might run into on the way! My trusty club and I could come in very handy."

Wen had extreme doubts about the trustiness of her club. Still, it probably wouldn't be very nice to leave her

17

stranded in a village where there was little to eat except dragon meat and with no way out except, perhaps, conjuring a pig or whatever she might manage with her crazy magic. "I suppose I can at least see you to the castle."

"Brilliant." Arrow swung herself up on Bay and settled behind Wen. She bounced twice on the saddle and wrapped her arms around him. Her breastplate pressed against his back and her helmet dug uncomfortably into his shoulder blade. "Ready!"

"Hup, Bay!" Wen nudged the horse lightly with his foot. Bay immediately set off at a canter.

It was a very short ride to the little pond nestled away from the town. Moonlight sparkled on the surface of the water and an owl hooted nearby as Wen brought Bay to a halt. Arrow was leaning heavily on Wen's back, and he waited for her to dismount.

When she didn't move, he said, "I'd like to sleep now. Arrow? Arrow." He twisted around and caught her as she started to fall off the horse. He slid off Bay and pulled Arrow down after him. Her eyes were closed in sleep and her helmet was askew.

Muttering under his breath about sorceresses and their eccentricities, Wen carried Arrow over to a grassy, flat area and set her down. He pulled her helmet the rest of the way off and placed it next to her. She mumbled something about glass carpets and rolled onto her stomach.

Wen then took off his belt and sword and tended to Bay, removing the saddlebags and all the riding gear. He spent a few minutes brushing his horse down and was about to spread his blanket on the ground when Bay trotted up to him and bumped Wen's back with his nose.

"What?" Wen turned to face his horse, his blanket in his hands.

Bay whinnied and ground one hoof into the dirt. He tossed his head very deliberately in Arrow's direction.

"I'm sure she's fine. Look, she's sleeping quite peacefully."

Bay huffed a breath of hot air right in Wen's face.

Wen rolled his eyes and grumbled under his breath, "Honestly, you are such a ladies' horse."

Bay nipped the blanket in Wen's hands, tugging it away

from him and shaking it in his teeth.

"All right, I get it!" Wen snatched the blanket back from Bay, walked over to Arrow, and draped it over her. "There. Satisfied?"

Bay tilted his head down toward the grass, so Wen took that as a yes.

"Bad enough growing up with two parents, six elder brothers, and a dozen tutors and nursemaids telling me what to do. Now I'm getting bossed around by a horse." Wen pulled a thick cloak from one of the saddlebags and spread it out so he could sleep on it. "This had better not become a usual thing. You know what happened to the last lady you were taken with. Do you want to get turned into a porcupine again?"

Bay shuddered as Wen lay on his cloak. "Yes, I didn't think so."

3 – Deal

Wen woke to something gripping his ankle and dragging him across the ground at a very rapid pace. His eyes snapped open and focused on a young woman who was so gorgeous she actually glowed in the moonlight. Long black hair flowed around her and her silky white dress revealed a voluptuous figure. She had him by the ankle, and her grasp was tighter than one of the carnivorous flytraps in his uncle's garden. His heart plunged to his toes in a very unpleasant way.

Wen flailed and kicked, and the vice around his ankle tightened so much he feared his bones would break. He clawed at the ground in a desperate attempt to stop himself. His fingers had nothing to grasp except cattail reeds, and he was pulled steadily toward the pond.

"Bay!" he shouted. His hands landed on a small rock. He picked it up and lobbed it at his captor's head. She caught it with the hand not holding his ankle and pinned icy blue eyes on him. She made a noise somewhere between a hiss and a growl and yanked him closer still to the water.

"Bay, I need my sword! There's a water nymph!" He was only meters away from the pond now. He had only ever heard horror stories of water nymphs—deceptively beautiful maidens who stole men they fancied to their watery homes. What happened to the men was widely disputed, as most never returned from an encounter with a nymph. The few who did came back insane and babbled nonsense.

Bay whinnied, and his hooves pounded across the ground toward Wen. Wen's sword landed right beside his arm as his boots touched the water's edge.

Getting the sword out of his scabbard was easy enough. Doing any damage to the nymph proved more difficult. He tried to hit her arm, to break her hold, but his sword bounced off as if she were made of thick sponge.

Bay had hold of Wen's shirt sleeve with his teeth and was doing his best to tug him back. Wen's legs were in the pond now, though he couldn't feel any water on his trousers or skin.

In his alarmed exhaustion and so used to traveling alone, Wen had forgotten that Bay wasn't the only one nearby until Arrow flipped neatly over his head and landed in the water, one leg planted on either side of him, her club pointed directly at the water nymph.

"Back off, you fiend!"

The nymph gave that horrible growling hiss, such a bizarre sound to come out of such a pretty face. She jerked Wen forward sharply, so he was in the water up to his chest and struggling to push himself up on his elbows before his face went under. Arrow didn't help the situation when she sat on his stomach and wrapped her legs underneath him, as if she thought that would anchor him in place.

"Let him go!" Arrow's club glowed brightly, and something burst from the end of it and smacked the nymph in the face. It was a giant, thick snake, and it swiftly wound itself around the nymph's face and neck. Wen doubted whether it was hurting the nymph at all, but it was covering her eyes and making it very hard for her to see.

The nymph's hiss turned into a shriek, and Arrow tried to beat the nymph around the shoulders with her club without hitting the snake. "Let"—*smack*—"him"—*thwack*—"go, you hussy!"

Wen had no idea if her club was making an impact or if it was bouncing off as his sword had. He had other concerns. There was a loud ripping noise as Wen was wrenched from Bay's grasp, leaving only a piece of shirt in the horse's teeth, and Wen was pulled straight under the water. The last thing he saw before his head sank under the surface was another flash of light from Arrow's club. He could still breathe, which was a very odd sensation, and his foot was numb from the hold the nymph still had on him.

Next moment, there came a loud, echoing shriek, and the fingers on his ankle disappeared. His clothes were instantly soaked, and his ability to breathe underwater vanished. He sucked in a lungful of water.

Arrow's weight shifted off of Wen's stomach, and she hauled him to the surface by the collar of his shirt. He hacked and coughed while Arrow shoved him toward the edge of the pond.

"Get out, get out, I don't know how long I stopped her!"

"How—?" He coughed some more and struggled to breathe as he slogged out of the water.

"Fire!" Arrow waggled her club triumphantly. "Water creatures can't stand fire. I hit her with a nice blast of it and she shot across to the other side of the pond. It's what I was trying to do when I set the snake on her. Come on, let's get away from this place *now*."

Wen wasn't about to argue. He hastily gathered up his belongings while Bay moved back and forth in front of the water like some kind of guard dog. Within thirty seconds, Wen, Arrow, and Bay were hightailing it away from the pond, Wen walking as best he could on his still half-numb foot.

"'Nice little pond,' indeed!" Arrow exclaimed. "Honestly, Wenceslas! You and your stupid handsome face, attracting a water nymph!"

"It's not like I asked her to come after me!"

"Tch."

Bay whickered and nudged first Wen and then Arrow with his nose, distracting Wen from any arguments he wanted to make.

Arrow melted and gushed over how brilliant Bay was, and Wen patted his flank and whispered, "Thanks, friend."

"I've never had to worry about water nymphs before," Arrow said. Then she suddenly grinned. The warm blue of her eyes was so different from the freezing blue of the water nymph's. "It was pretty amazing, though, wasn't it? Did you *see* the size of that snake!?"

"I thought that was an accident," Wen said grumpily. He was a little shaken by how close the water nymph had come to stealing him away, and he was soaked from head to toe for the second time that night.

Arrow waved away this comment. "Told you I'd come in handy," she said smugly. She hummed happily as they went along until they found a clearing far away from any water. She pulled off her sodden boots and removed her breastplate.

Wen sat down to take off his boots. He dumped the water out of them and squeezed more out of his tunic. At least the pond had washed away any remaining traces of smells and dragon bits. He looked up when he saw a flash of light that indicated Arrow was using her club, and he tried not to wince when he found it pointed at him. Half a dozen bats appeared and flew off into the night. Arrow's face squinted in concentration, and next moment, Wen was completely dry.

"There!" Arrow lowered her club and patted her now dry hair. "Much better. Good night, Wenceslas darling."

His eyebrows shot up. *Darling?*

She didn't seem to notice the odd look he was giving her. She promptly dropped to the ground, rolled again onto her stomach, and was asleep before Wen had even laid out his cloak. Before Bay could poke and prod him about it, Wen tossed his blanket over Arrow.

"I don't know how she can sleep," he muttered to Bay. He stretched out on his back and tried to get his muscles to relax. "I tell you what, Bay, I'd take the flying crocs in our moat at home over a water nymph any day."

***

The castle in the center of town was one of the tiniest Wen had ever seen. It looked rather like the birthday cake he had tried to make one year for his mother: squat and with a tower that tilted slightly to one side. Green ivy crept up the walls and hung along the roof. A few servants were wandering the small grounds and battling with the weed-ridden, overgrown gardens. They seemed to be losing.

"Does this castle look a little rundown to you?" Arrow peered around Wen from the back of Bay's saddle. Her arms hung loosely around Wen's middle. "I mean, even two years in magicked sleep shouldn't have made it quite like this, right?"

Wen eyed the sagging castle doubtfully. "I'm sure it will be lovely with a little caretaking."

He brought Bay to a halt in front of the path leading up to the castle. One gardener was hacking through the winding creepers and leaves that crisscrossed the path. Wen climbed off Bay and reached back for Arrow. She slid down, and he caught her by the hips and set her on the ground.

Her eyes sparkled as she peered up at him. "You know, I can get off a horse by myself."

"You can leap on dragons and do flips while wearing a breastplate and helmet," Wen returned. "I've no doubt you're capable of dismounting a horse."

"If you're just going to be all good manners and whatnot, very well." Arrow curtsied, surprisingly graceful in her trousers and breastplate. Her helmet was tied to Wen's saddlebag. She hooked her arm through Wen's and then ruined her poise by skipping toward the path as she dragged Wen along with her.

They quickly reached the gardener on the path. He was dripping sweat as he beat at the weeds with a small garden scythe.

"Allow me to help, good sir." Wen disentangled his arm from Arrow's. He had his sword half out of its scabbard when Arrow whipped out her club.

"That will take forever. I've got this." She waved her club, and it began to glow. "I'll just slice a path...er. Oh."

Across the lawn and gardens, every single plant and weed—including the grass—had suddenly turned to feathers. They blew around in the light breeze, and Arrow sneezed as some drifted past her nose. The servants all stood frozen in piles of feathers. The one in front of them held his scythe up, his mouth agape.

Arrow cleared her throat. "At least the plants are out of the way!"

"Magic!" The gardener at last found his voice. "Begone, you witch! We've had enough spells here to last a lifetime!"

"I am *not* a witch." Arrow planted her hands on her hips, her club sticking out at an angle. "I am a sorceress. Witches and wizards deal more in potions and powders and memorizing spells and stuff like that. Sorceresses and sorcerers use some of that, but they deal primarily in creating spells, studying, and utilizing how magic flows all around us. There's *schooling* and *theory* involved. There is a difference."

The gardener's face reddened, and Wen quickly reclaimed Arrow's arm and tugged her forward, kicking up clouds of feathers as he skirted around the angry servant.

"I don't think he's very interested in the difference," he said as they approached the castle's front doors. The doors were wooden and gilded with faded metalwork, as if once upon a time they had been pretty but were now in the same sad state as the rest of the castle.

"Tch." Arrow's tsking noise was grumpy. "Witch, indeed. Wenceslas," she said suddenly, her head tilting up to take in the length of the castle, "what is your castle like? Is it small like this?"

"Oh, no. It's huge. It's really very beautiful. It's made of white stone and it has a lot of crystal and glass in windows and turrets, and when the sun strikes it, the whole thing glitters—rather like the ocean our castle overlooks." He pulled the bell rope, and a bell within the house gonged loudly. Moments later, the front doors creaked open and a hassled-looking woman squinted out at them.

"Yes?"

Wen bowed. "I'm Wenceslas, seventh prince of Eirdane, come to see the good rulers of this fair land. This is my companion, Arrow, sorceress of—" He paused, not having any idea where Arrow came from.

"Nayrlanda," Arrow supplied.

Wen shot her a quick look of surprise, and the woman bowed to them in a harried way. "Come in, your lord and ladyship. King Pompholiontius and his daughter are dining at the moment. I will inform them you've arrived. I would offer you chairs, but I've not yet finished dusting the sitting room."

"Wenceslas, this is a very bad idea," Arrow muttered as the servant bustled off through a door. "Do you see this place? There are no pictures. No tapestries or paintings or sculptures—no *life*. It's all drab and gray and bland, and do you *really* want to have a father-in-law named Pamphlet—"

"Pompholiontius."

"—Pamphlet Lion Chest?"

"Pomph—oh, never mind. Listen, I'll admit this isn't the best castle I've ever been to—"

"It's not about whether it's a castle or not," Arrow interrupted. "I've seen tents more hospitable than this. It's just—it's the lack of personality. It's so *unfeeling* here."

The servant woman returned before Wen could respond. She ushered Wen and Arrow into a long, dusty dining hall. Several more servants dotted the edge of the room, and seated at the table were the king and princess. The king was an old man who wore a varnished crown on his white-and-yellow hair. He looked at them with tired, droopy eyes that reminded Wen of his third eldest brother's hound dogs. The princess had the same droopy hound dog eyes and hair the color of straw. She was also about twice Wen's age.

Wen bowed and Arrow curtseyed. Wen swallowed and prepared to make introductions, but Arrow beat him to it.

"Your highnesses, welcome to the land of awake people! I'm Arrow, sorceress of Nayrlanda, and this is Prince Window Glass."

Wen barely resisted the urge to slap his forehead.

"We just wanted to let you know that we have slain the dragon to which your sleeping spell was tied, and you and your kingdom are free! So enjoy your lives, eat well, and consider adding some color around here. Some flowers, maybe some rugs—I know this fantastic weaver over in the town of Lorshire, if you want her name."

"No, thank you," the king said in a voice as tired as his eyes. "We are quite happy with our castle as it is, aren't we, my dear?"

The princess nodded, though she didn't seem terribly interested one way or another.

"We'll be leaving now," Arrow said graciously. She curtseyed again and took a step backward toward the door.

"Arrow," Wen murmured, "I have to at least *try.*"

"No. No, you don't have to *try,* not for this," Arrow whispered back. "I have a better idea. Come on." She took his hand and tugged him toward the door.

Wen was torn between what might be worse: trying to marry this princess or what one of Arrow's ideas might consist of. He glanced back at the princess, who stifled a yawn and poked listlessly at her food.

Arrow's fingers were insistent on his, and it was the lively way she was rolling back and forth on her heels, as if she were ready to skip or dance or leap at a moment's notice, that prompted his decision. He'd take his chances with bubbly Arrow rather than force himself to possibly marry an apathetic woman old enough to be his mother.

He bowed to the king and princess and went with Arrow. She beamed, dropped his hand, and led the way back through the castle and out through the piles of feathers being swept up by the gardeners. It wasn't until they had reached Bay that Wen asked, "All right, so what was this idea of yours?"

"Keep looking," Arrow said. "May I?" She pointed at the pocket on his saddlebag filled with oats, and Wen nodded. "I think," she continued, pulling out a handful of oats and offering it to Bay, "that you should keep looking for an enchanted princess for the next few weeks, like you have been. You can't just *settle* on anyone, Wenceslas; you have to fight for what you want. Look for a princess you might actually *want* to spend the rest of your life with."

"And if I don't find the right princess in the next few weeks and I prick my finger on a glass coffin?" Wen asked gloomily.

Bay ate the oats out of Arrow's hand, and Arrow patted his nose absently. "Then I promise you that I will find some fun, colorful, smart girl and tell her what a wonderful person you are. I won't rest until I convince her that she's your true love, and she kisses you and you wake up." She dusted her hand off on her trousers. "Some enchantments are tricky or impossible to get around, but you can't let them run your life. There's always a second option. You just have to look for it. So what do you say?"

"I say I've been wandering around trying to break this enchantment for four years and I haven't met the right princess for me. Three weeks doesn't seem like a lot of time to do it."

"Ah, but you've never traveled with *me* before. Enchantments are my specialty, remember?" Arrow stuck out her hand. "Three weeks to find the woman you *want* to spend the rest of your life with, or I swear I will get you out of that enchanted sleep. Deal?"

Arrow stood there with such confidence that Wen nodded slowly. He grasped Arrow's hand and they shook on it. "Deal."

"How do you usually go about finding enchanted princesses?" Arrow swung up onto Bay's saddle. She scooted forward. Wen clambered up behind her and allowed her to take the reins.

"Sometimes I listen to stories from villagers or defeated heroes," Wen said. "Sometimes I stop by taverns and look at their notice boards. People are always posting pleas for help."

"There's a much faster way. We can go to Nayrlanda; the university gets dozens of people seeking help for enchantments every day. That's going to be our best bet."

"Yes, Nayrlanda," Wen said. The best sorcerers and sorceresses of the world had come out of Nayrlanda University. "You *trained* there?"

"Sort of," Arrow said hesitantly. He couldn't see her expression; he gazed down at the top of her head and waited. She squirmed restlessly. "It's complicated."

"More complicated than my drunken fairy godmother giftcurse?" he asked wryly.

"Let's just say the university and I didn't always see eye to eye."

Wen wondered how much of that had to do with her magic constantly going awry.

"It shouldn't take too long to get there," Arrow said. "Probably three or four days from here. Ready?"

"Ready."

Arrow nudged Bay into motion. "I should probably warn you that we might have to sneak into the university once we get there."

"Part of that complicated story you're not telling me?"

"Maybe."

"I still don't even know your real name."

"You can still just call me Arrow."

"Ever the mystery, aren't you, Arrow?"

Arrow tilted her head back so she could see him and fluttered her lashes at him. "What fun would it be if I didn't have a mystery or two about me?"

4 – Tisi Forest

"Wenceslas! Wenceslas, wake up!"

Wen cracked open his eyes only because Arrow was poking a finger into his rib cage repeatedly.

"Honestly, Arrow, can't we get *one* decent night of sleep? Three nights ago, it was the water nymph. Two nights ago, it was a very loud inn. Last night, it was that blasted ogre."

"Now it's a forest. Wake *up!*"

Wen sat up with a groan that was immediately cut off when he understood what Arrow was talking about. "I don't recall falling asleep in a forest."

"That's because we *didn't.*"

Wen stood. He and Arrow were in a clearing surrounded by thick trees. The first rays of sunrise filtered through branches. A cool breeze brushed across his cheeks and carried the smell of something faintly exotic. Cinnamon? Everything was a little too colorful—the leaves were a little too green and tinted with blue here and there. The brown of the bark was deeper and richer than that of ordinary trees, and even the chirps of the birds sounded sweeter than normal. A dirt path led away from their clearing, twisting through the woods.

"Tisi Forest," he said wonderingly.

"Yes." Arrow straightened from her crouch. "Have you ever been here?"

"No, I've only heard the stories." Wen stepped past Bay and ran a hand gently over the tree nearest him. The smell of cinnamon grew stronger.

"Careful!" Arrow grabbed his hand and pulled it away from the tree. "You never know which trees in here might have wood sprites or be enchanted or something." She let go of him and spun in a slow circle. "I'm a little surprised you haven't been here before, being under that giftcurse your whole life. Tisi Forest draws magicked or magic people into itself. Or it appears where those people are. There are tremendously long debates at Nayrlanda University about this place and how it works. No one's ever decided definitively."

"I suppose the forest never thought it needed me to be here before. Have *you* ever been here?"

"No, but my elder brother, Algernon, got stuck here for six months once. It was one disaster after another for him. My younger brother, Reginald, on the other hand, was here for two days and everything was fantastic for him."

"How many brothers do you have?" Wen crouched down to get a good look at some brilliant orange and pink flowers blossoming at the base of a tree.

"Just the two. And two sisters—one elder, one younger. My sisters have never been here, though. I looked for this place once, but Tisi Forest apparently didn't think I needed to be here, either."

Arrow turned and began to break up their small camp, and Wen joined her. Afterward, they ate a quick breakfast, and Arrow threw instructions out at Wen. "Don't drink from any water in here until we check that it's not bespelled. Algernon got himself turned into a goat once while he was here because of that. And if we run across any hags, for the love of dragons, don't insult them."

"Arrow," Wen said patiently, "I've been around my share of enchantments. I'm not stupid."

"Right, right. I know you're not. Sorry, it's just that at the university, we get a lot of really *stupid* princes—mostly first and second sons, mind you—coming in for help. I spent two months in records, which meant I got to write down their sob stories, and most of them would have been perfectly fine if they'd had an ounce of common sense. Loads of fun, let me tell you. Turn around, I'm going to change."

Wen quickly turned.

"I figure," Arrow said, amid a lot of rustling clothes, "that the more I look like a damsel in distress, the easier this place will be to get through. From what I hear, Tisi

30

Forest is much kinder to damsels in distress than it is to idiots who stick their noses into every enchantment they can manage here. *Algernon*," she muttered under her breath. "There, I'm dressed."

She wore a plain blue dress that brought out the color of her eyes. "Do you think I'll look all damsel-in-distress-like if I put my breastplate back on?"

"I think you'd have trouble looking like a damsel in distress no matter what you're wearing," Wen said. "Especially with that club dangling from your hip. You *do* look lovely."

Arrow flashed him a quick smile. "Bet you I can play the damsel in distress if I need to."

"Bet you can, too," he said. "And then probably whack some poor, unsuspecting sap with your magic club when his back is turned."

"My club's not magic in itself. It's only magic enhancing," Arrow corrected.

"You could still whack him with it." He considered her. "Arrow isn't a very damsel-in-distress sort of name, you know."

"Wenceslas, are you still trying to wheedle my name out of me?" Arrow shook her finger at him. "It's not going to work. Besides, do you really think most princes or heroes would give half a copper what my name is? In the two months I did records at the university, I had numerous couples who came in to file marriage agreements. Many of them had met in the 'you broke my enchantment, so I'm madly in love with you' sort of way. In three cases, they didn't even know each other's names." She began to saddle Bay, and Wen moved to help her. "I'm making an addition to my promise to you. If you fall into an enchanted sleep and I have to convince a girl she's your true love, I assure you that she will know your name."

"Fantastic. So which name will I wake up to? Winces Lots or Window Glass?"

"Neither, silly prince," Arrow said airily. "Wen Says Lots, of course." She smirked at him as they stepped back from Bay. "We need to do something about your clothes now." She fingered her club.

Wen held out both hands in protest. "Excuse me, but

31

the last time you tried to do something about my clothes, I ended up green and in a towel."

"No, darling, the last time I tried to do something about your clothes, they ended up *dry* and still in place."

Wen wasn't fazed by her 'darling' comment this time; after he'd heard her call an old man *and* a little girl in the inn 'darling,' he'd realized she said it to everybody. "After you conjured bats."

Arrow waved this off. "I don't need my club for this one, anyway." She crouched down and swiped her fingers along the dirt on the ground. "Your best chance is going to be the humble woodcutter." She stretched onto her tiptoes and smeared dirt on his cheeks. "Humble woodcutters have a tremendous success rate of getting magical gifts and avoiding trouble."

"Arrow," he said, standing very still because allowing her to rub dirt on his face was a lot better than having her club aimed at him, "do you honestly think a magic forest is going to be fooled by either of us disguising ourselves as something we're not?"

"No, but the people *in* the forest might be fooled." Arrow rubbed more dirt on his shirt. Her small hands sliding down his chest sent tingles through his body—and then he stifled a shout of laughter as her fingers hit a very ticklish spot. "We're not going to *lie* to anyone. Lying about who you are is the fastest way to end up in a nasty spell."

Wen shuddered. "Believe me, I've heard unpleasant stories about that."

"We're just going to try to avoid immediately being spotted as a sorceress and a prince. Try not to stand as straight, all right? Slouch a little bit here and there."

Wen forced his shoulders down.

"That's pathetic," Arrow said.

"Hey, you try having lessons on posture throughout your childhood and then slouch on command!"

"All right." Arrow's shoulders drooped and she hunched over like a sad little waif. "There. My mother would have fits if she saw me like this."

The more Arrow mentioned her family and upbringing, the more curious Wen was about who she was and how she had ended up roaming the world hunting for enchantments to study.

Wen climbed on Bay's saddle and reached his hand down toward Arrow. "Perchance, lovely damsel, will you allow this humble woodcutter to escort you through this magic forest?"

Arrow took Wen's hand and let him pull her up in front of him. She sat sideways because of her dress and spoke in a breathy voice, the sort that he'd heard numerous times from a lot of princesses. "Lead on, oh humble woodcutter, for I know not what I would doest—"

"Doest?"

"Shut up, I'm making a damsel in distress speech," she said in her regular voice before switching back to the breathy one. "I know not what I would doest if thou didn'tst—"

"That is *not* a word."

"Shh! Didn'tst rescue me on thy beautiful steed." Arrow put the back of her hand to her forehead in a swoon.

Wen gave a snort of laughter. "Hup, Bay." He patted Bay's neck and Bay jolted into motion. "Carefully, all right, boy? Let's stick to the path."

Arrow settled against Wen as Bay picked his way down the path. It was almost unnaturally smooth. The very air seemed to be holding its breath, as if waiting for something to happen.

"Can you feel it?" Arrow whispered. "Everything in here is crackling, like a spark could set it off and make the whole thing explode with magic. It's beautiful and terrifying."

"I can't really feel it, but I'm not surprised."

The sun had risen fully and shone down through the trees, making everything it touched glitter and sparkle. A few times, Wen was sure he caught glimpses of motion in the woods, but every time he tried to look more closely, whatever it was had vanished. The only company he, Bay, and Arrow had was the songbirds that flitted from tree to tree and an occasional squirrel or rabbit that darted across the path into the underbrush.

"How big do you think Tisi Forest is?" Wen asked.

"I don't know," Arrow said. "Again, that's another huge debate at the university. Personally, after listening to my brothers' stories and a lot of other stories from people who

33

have come through here, I think that it holds you for as long as you need to be held and the size is inconsequential. Maybe we're here to learn something, or to help someone, or get help from someone else. I don't know where we'll come out. Probably somewhere we need to be, unless we do lots of stupid things while we're here, like Algernon did. After his six months here, he came out in the far north near a glacier. Had a bang-up time getting home." She looked up at Wen. "I shouldn't be so down on him. Algernon is a fabulous sorcerer. He poked his big nose into enchantments here because he wanted to study them. My brother Reginald was on a much more specific quest when he came here. We—do you hear that?"

A faint but very familiar sound reached Wen's ears. "It sounds like a baby crying."

Arrow tilted her head. "It's definitely a baby crying. Or something that sounds like a baby crying. Bay, can you take us to it?"

Bay neighed and picked up his pace as if to prove how well he could track down the baby's wails. The shrieks grew louder and louder as Bay trotted along the path. They rounded a curve and came upon a small, thatched cottage. Bay stopped in front of a well outside of it.

The crying was definitely coming from the cottage. Arrow slipped off of Bay and Wen leapt down after her. "It's probably just some family whose baby is hungry or upset," she whispered.

"In this place, it could also be some demented witch who's stolen someone's baby," Wen murmured back.

Together, they moved to the front door. Wen looked at Arrow. She nodded, and he knocked firmly.

Footsteps came near and the door was flung open. Wen and Arrow looked down. An extremely short, bearded man jostled a very unhappy baby in one arm. His eyes were bloodshot, and he tugged frantically on his beard, which was missing half its whiskers.

"What do you want? I'm not in the market for more gold work! Don't you see I have my hands full!?"

"You have a sweet baby," Arrow said.

The baby's face was scrunched up in misery and red from screaming. He didn't *look* very sweet.

34

The little man seemed to agree. "Sweet? *Sweet?* Do you know how much sleep I've had this week?" He pulled at his beard again and tugged out several more whiskers. "Who knew babies cried so much?"

Arrow held out her arms. "May I?"

The little man thrust the baby into Arrow's arms. Arrow shifted him up against her shoulder and rubbed his back, murmuring soothing nonsense. Almost immediately, the baby stopped screeching.

The little man fell face first on the ground and moaned in relief. "Oh, lucky stars! I thought he would never stop. Thank you, fair maiden, *thank you!*"

"Isn't his mother around?" Arrow asked.

"His mother! She's the one who started this whole mess." The man dragged himself off of the floor and slumped back into the cottage. "Come in, come in. Least I can do is offer you some tea."

Wen and Arrow stepped cautiously inside. The little man began to brew tea at a tiny stove and set out three teacups. He motioned for Wen and Arrow to sit at the table, which was so miniscule that Wen had to sit on his knees on the floor so he wouldn't risk breaking a chair. Arrow was small enough to perch on the edge of a chair.

"Thank you very much for your hospitality," Arrow said politely.

The little man carried the tea and a plate of biscuits to the table. He pulled out a flask and dumped a generous amount of whiskey into his teacup. He drank it down quickly.

"Name's Stiltskin, Rumpel Stiltskin. That's the prince heir of Idlin." Rumpel nodded at the baby, who had fallen sound asleep on Arrow's shoulder. "Not a week old, and I'm going to go mad, I am, taking care of him."

"Did his mother get lost in the forest?" Wen asked.

Rumpel gave a huge snort. "Lost! The only thing that woman's lost is her brains! Ohhh, how did I get myself into this?" He poured another cup of tea with more whiskey and downed that, too.

Wen took a sip of the tea. His polite upbringing and his fear that turning down a gift would land him with a terrible curse kept him drinking it despite how strong and bitter it was.

"It started with the miller of Idlin. Foolish man got it in his head to tell people his daughter could spin straw into gold. I'm a gold-spinner, see—learned from my grandma. I went to Idlin to see what was what, and I'd only just got there when the king of Idlin nabbed the girl and threatened her with death if she didn't change a whole room of straw into gold! Well, I didn't think it was fair to let the girl die because her pa was an idiot."

"You spun the straw to gold for her?" Arrow asked. "That was very kind of you."

"It didn't come without a price. Part of the magic of gold-spinning, see. I'm bound to get compensation for the spinning. So she gave me this necklace she had. Good enough for me, I says, so I fix all the straw up for her. Except then the king wants her to do it *again* the next night. I'd like to spin him to gold, I would," Rumpel muttered darkly, pouring a third cup of whiskey tea. "Well, I couldn't just leave the miller girl crying, could I?"

Arrow and Wen shook their heads. Arrow picked up a biscuit and nibbled on it while Rumpel continued, "So she gave me her ring and I spun the straw. The problem came the *third* night. The king gave her more straw to spin, and the girl was all out of trinkets. She promised me she'd give me her firstborn child if I'd just help her one more time. What, I ask you, was I going to do with a child? She had to have *something* else to offer. Only thing she had was her clothes, and I wasn't going to leave her naked! So I agreed, fine, she could give me her firstborn. Figured I'd find a way out of it if that ever came to pass."

Wen's eyes flickered over to the baby.

"So then the king goes and *marries* the girl, and not a year later, this one's born!" Rumpel tipped back his third drink. "I was here at home, working in my garden, calm as you please, and then suddenly I'm at the palace, faced with a weeping queen, begging me not to take her baby. But I was magic-bound to do it! Can't break my own magic, can I? Grandmother who taught me gold-spinning was a fairy godmother, you know."

Wen groaned. "You used fairy godmother magic to do the gold-spinning?"

"I'm not a proper fairy *anything*, of course," Rumpel said, "but I can't ignore the rules. I tell her, all right, I can tack an addendum on there. If you can guess my name in three days, you can keep your baby. Figured that would work, right? I even went out of my way to make sure she would find out what it was. I wore a nametag on my hat! I made sure her servants were following me and I danced around a fire singing out my name! But one of her servants was turned into a newt by the neighborhood witch and one of them was eaten by a troll. So here I am, stuck with a baby, and all I want to do is *sleep!*"

Arrow laid the baby gently on her lap. His tiny face was peaceful in slumber. "Mr. Stiltskin, can't you simply give the baby back to his mother, now that he's yours to do with as you please?"

"I tried. The magic wouldn't let me, since the deal was between me and his mother. As soon as I left the baby in the castle, he reappeared right in my arms!" Rumpel's face hit the table and he moaned. "What I am going to do?"

"There's always a second option," Arrow whispered. Her eyes flicked over to Wen. "Even with fairy godmother magic. Some people don't find it, but it's always there."

"What second option?" Rumpel's voice was muffled by the table.

"Give him to us," Wen said suddenly.

Arrow shot him a look of surprise. "I was about to say that."

Rumpel looked up. "Give him...to you?"

"Yes. If you can't give him directly to his mother, then give him to us," Wen said. "And we'll give him back to you—" Horror dawned on Rumpel's face, and Wen hurriedly finished, "And we'll tell you to give him back to his mother. Do you think that will fulfill the magic?"

"Well," Rumpel said slowly, "there's one way to find out." He stood. "I hereby bequeath this baby to—I'm sorry, what are your names? I'll need them for this to even possibly work."

"You can just give the baby to him," Arrow said quickly. "Wenceslas, seventh prince of Eirdane."

"I hereby bequeath this baby to Wenceslas, seventh prince of Eirdane, to do with as he sees fit."

Arrow drew in a sharp breath and rubbed her ears. "Something *popped.* I think that worked. Wenceslas?"

"And I hereby bequeath this baby to his mother—" Wen paused.

Rumpel Stiltskin said, "Charlotte von Rimmenstein."

"—Charlotte von Rimmenstein, to be delivered to her by Rumpel Stiltskin." He glanced at Arrow, who nodded at him.

"Let's see if that worked." Rumpel stood and gathered up the baby in Arrow's lap. "I'll be back in a few minutes. Help yourself to the tea and biscuits."

He carried the baby out the door, and Arrow grabbed another biscuit.

Rumpel Stiltskin was as good as his word. He was back a few minutes later, without the baby. He stepped cautiously back through his door and peered around.

"I've never come this far without the baby reappearing after I left him with his mother." Rumpel looked as though he hardly dared believe that he might really be free. He crept over to the table and sat down. They waited in silence for several more minutes, but there was still no baby.

Finally, Rumpel let out a huge breath and sagged in his seat. "It worked. Bless my lucky stars, it *worked.* Thank you! Thank you both! I don't know how I can ever repay you!"

"Please, no need for repayment." Wen had no desire to have anything to do with whatever shreds of fairy godmother magic Rumpel Stiltskin possessed.

"Then allow me to at least give you some friendly advice," Rumpel said. "I imagine if you're in the forest, you have a reason for being here, but proceed with caution. Never touch the yellow flowers. If a bird speaks to you, don't answer him. If you happen upon a bog, try to go far around it. And please, take some biscuits with you."

Arrow rose and Wen followed suit. Once Arrow had accepted the biscuits, they thanked Rumpel Stiltskin and left his house. Wen got a last glimpse of Rumpel downing a fourth whiskey tea before he closed the door.

5 – Troll Crossing

"That baby reminded me of my niece and nephews when they were little," Arrow said as they rode Bay away from Rumpel's house. "Delphina—my elder sister—has three children."

"Five of my brothers are married, and four of them have children. I have eight nieces, four nephews, and two more on the way," Wen replied.

"Aw, I bet you're a great uncle."

"The children are a lot of fun." Wen looked down at the top of Arrow's head. "So, your brothers are Algernon and Reginald, and your elder sister is Delphina. What's your younger sister's name?"

"Elisabette. She's ten."

"And what's your name?"

"Ha. Nice try." Arrow leaned comfortably back against him. "Names are powerful things, you know."

"Yes, I think we just proved that with Rumpel Stiltskin back there. Why are you so concerned with keeping yours secret?" he asked.

"Ah, it's not that I want to keep it a secret. As I said before, it's complicated."

"Try me."

"Biscuit?" Arrow held one out to him. She waited until he took it, and then stuffed another one in her mouth, pointedly bringing their conversation to a halt.

They soon ran across a large sign that read: TROLL CROSSING – NEXT 6 KILOMETERS.

"Ugh, trolls," Arrow said. "I certainly hope we don't meet any."

39

"Me, too. I don't know how much more my shield can take." Wen eyed the dented shield strapped to Bay's saddle.

Bay whickered and picked up his pace, clearly not wanting to meet any trolls if he could help it, either. Arrow slid her club out of its sheath and held it across her lap. She and Wen jumped when a blur of feathers zoomed down nearly onto Arrow's head. It swerved and flew around them once, then settled on one of the saddlebags, talons digging into the cloth. It had brilliantly colored plumage, like a rainbow on wings.

"Travelers!" the bird squawked. "Good day to you!"

Wen and Arrow exchanged glances, and neither of them answered the bird. Wen was grateful they'd received Rumpel's advice, because who knew what would happen if they talked to the bird? There were a dozen possibilities, none of which Wen particularly wanted to experience.

"I said, good day to you!" the bird repeated.

They remained silent. Wen wondered if he should dare try to scare the bird away, or if that would get him cursed. He decided the best thing to do would be to just ignore it entirely.

The bird's voice turned mournful. "Ahh! Why stay silent, friends? I only desire some cheering conversation!"

Arrow tilted her head, studying the bird, and leaned so close to it that Wen had to resist the urge to grab the back of her dress to keep her from falling off the saddle. He reminded himself that she wasn't an ordinary maiden and definitely not a damsel in distress, and that she was more than capable of staying on Bay without assistance.

"Alas, sweet maiden, kind maiden, won't you do me the great honor of speaking with me?" the bird asked.

Arrow straightened and looked at Wen. She said, only to him, "Wenceslas, this bird is under some kind of enchantment. I can feel it—it's kind of a burning sensation in my middle. Whatever it is, it's not very nice."

"Ah!" the bird half gasped, half squawked. "How your intellect shines, but not greater than your beauty!"

"It could be that we have to ask it about its enchantment or it won't be able to tell us," Arrow said thoughtfully.

The bird raised its wings in an excited sort of motion and flapped them once before settling them against its back

40

again. "Oh, brilliant maiden, lovely maiden! How—"

"Or," Arrow interrupted the bird, "perhaps if I were to speak to it directly, I would turn into a bird and it would turn back into whatever it was before."

The bird made a noise between a squawk and a choke, and Arrow's whole body tensed against Wen's. She pointed her club at the bird. A faint glow flowed over it, and she nodded. "Yes, that's it. Wenceslas, it's a switching spell. I've seen it before. A shape-shifting spell is cast on someone, and they can't change back unless they can get someone to take their place. The most common switching spells are activated by touch or by talk."

"I thought most shape-shifting spells are simply broken."

"Most are," Arrow agreed. "But sometimes you get a really sadistic witch or wizard who just wants the shape-shifting to be passed on instead of broken. It's a horrible thing to do to someone."

"Yes!" the bird exclaimed. "Yes, a horrible, terrible—"

Arrow's voice grew steely. "But I'm wondering what sort of person would be so desperate to break an enchantment that he would willingly place his curse on someone else."

If a bird could cry, this one burst into tears. The bird-like crying noises it made were horrible. "Ah, alas, alas! I have been in this form for too long to recount! I wish to leave this accursed place and return to my family. My bride-to-be must be frantic with worry! Please, please, have mercy! Have mercy! Being a bird has its advantages! You could fly!"

"Could you use magic to take it off of him without taking it on yourself?" Wen asked Arrow, almost unable to believe he was suggesting she use magic.

The bird immediately stopped its dreadful crying noises and turned its beady eyes toward Arrow.

"Today's magic lesson: Magic can rebound if you try to break it without fulfilling the spell's requirements. I mean, it's not impossible to break—this isn't fairy godmother magic—but it can be tricky. Don't worry." Arrow gave him a smug smile. "We don't need to take it off him; we only need—ahh!" She grabbed Wen, who clung hard to Bay's reins as Bay whinnied, reared onto his hind legs, and almost threw them off.

The cause of Bay's distress towered in front of them.

41

Twice as tall as Wen and three times as wide, the troll raised its arms and roared. Its ugly, squashed, green face contorted with rage. It swiped at Bay with long, sharp claws and just missed eviscerating him.

Arrow flung herself off Bay, and Wen leapt after her, drawing his sword as Arrow waved her club. He swiftly unhooked his shield from the saddle and slid his arm through the handle.

"Back!" Arrow shouted at the troll. "You're not eating that horse!"

The troll roared at Arrow, showing its sharp, pointed teeth. Arrow stood her ground and her club began to glow. Wen took advantage of the troll's attention on Arrow to leap behind it and jump on its back, aiming to stab the soft, fleshy spot behind its neck. The troll bucked, and Wen's sword slipped and slammed instead into the hard, leathery skin of its back, which did absolutely no damage. If Arrow had done any magic, it hadn't had any effect that he could see.

The bird squawked and flapped its wings, but it continued to cling to the saddlebag.

There was a loud cry from somewhere off to the side. Wen's attention was caught by a tall man with golden hair standing on the branch of a tree. Where had he come from?

"Never fear, fair maiden!" the stranger shouted. "I'll rescue you!" He grabbed the branch, swung himself down, and leapt forward toward the troll.

The troll backhanded the man and sent him flying into a nearby tree, where he collapsed, groaning.

Bay shied backward. The colorful bird let go of the saddlebag and zipped around the troll's head. The troll tried to snatch it out of the air and just missed. Wen, clinging to the back of the troll, aimed for its neck again. As he thrust his sword forward, the troll roared at the bird—and suddenly, Wen was falling through thin air, his sword pointed downward, right toward Arrow's stomach.

A flash of panic clenched his insides, and he twisted in an attempt to avoid stabbing Arrow. The side of his body slammed into her and she went down with an *"oomph!"* and then an *"OW!"* as he crashed on her legs. He cringed backward when he realized his hand was centimeters from touching a large, yellow flower.

"I'm sorry!" Wen leapt to his feet and pulled Arrow up, swiveling around to make sure there was no troll. It was gone. A young man with raven black hair stood nearby, and the colorful bird flew around their heads.

Wen and Arrow stared between the man and the bird. The man, maybe a few years older than them, held up his hands and wiggled his fingers, and then ran his hands through his hair.

"I'm free!" he shouted. "I'm *free!*" He darted over to Wen and shook his shoulder enthusiastically. "I'm free! I'm free!" He grabbed Arrow and lifted her off the ground, but promptly dropped her when she smacked him upside the head with her hand.

"You had better be very glad," she told him severely, shaking her club at him, "that your spell switched with a troll and not with one of us. You don't hug someone you were trying to turn into a bird or you will get slapped!"

The man fell to his knees, and his eyes filled with tears. "My lady! My kind, gentle lady!"

Wen put his sword in its sheath and kept a wary eye on the trees for signs of more trolls.

"You have no idea what it's like, being under such a curse for so long!" The man groveled at Arrow's feet. "Ahh! Alas! My—"

"I don't care," Arrow said. "Yes, it was a horrid person who cast the original switching spell, but trading your freedom for another's imprisonment is very dishonorable. You see that troll?" She pointed up at the bird flying in an angry and confused way over their heads. "That was your second option. Find something that deserves to be turned into a bird, not unwary travelers! You probably could have found a squirrel and made it chatter at you if you'd used your brain and thought it through! Now get away from me before I curse you with something else!"

The man fled into the forest, and, as if it had finally decided what to do, the enchanted troll bird dove after him, pecking at his head. Once they had vanished from sight, Wen raised his eyebrows at Arrow. Her face was flushed and her eyes sparked dangerously.

The other man, the golden-haired one who had come

out of nowhere, was still crumpled against a tree. Arrow walked over to him and bent down to check him. "He's breathing. I think he's just knocked out."

Wen moved over toward Bay, who was still stomping and rolling his eyes frantically. "It's all right, Bay, the troll is gone. It's all right."

Arrow put away her club and walked over to Bay. She wrapped her arms around his nose and nuzzled his face, and the angry flush of her cheeks started to fade. "My best friend when I was little found a talking turtle in a pond. I was with her. We were only six and didn't know about switching spells. She talked to it and poof! She was a turtle and there was a man about my father's age standing there."

"You must have been scared," Wen said.

"A bit. At first, I thought the turtle had turned Penelope into an old man, until the turtle started screaming my name. And the man—he just laughed and ran away. I, of course, told Penelope that I would take her right up to my father—"

"—and then you were the turtle?"

"Yes. Not very fun. Penelope left me there at the pond to go get my father, and in the end, he was able to free me from my wee turtle body." Arrow pursed her lips. "I was so angry when I understood that the man had tricked Penelope so he could be free." She dug a flask of water out of a saddlebag and carried it toward the unconscious man who had barged into the battle.

Assured that Bay was calm again, Wen followed her and knelt beside the stranger. "Where do you think he came from?"

"The tree," Arrow said in a patient voice. "Honestly, Wenceslas, how am I supposed to know? This is a magic forest." She threw water on the golden-haired man's face.

The man spluttered and sat bolt upright. "Never fear, I—" He stopped and blinked at Wen and Arrow. "Oh. Has the troll already been vanquished, then?"

"In a manner of speaking," Arrow said.

The man's shoulders slumped. "I failed in saving you, fair maiden. Please forgive me."

"Considering I didn't ask for you to save me, I have no idea why you're apologizing. Who are you?" Arrow asked.

The man flourished his hand toward himself. "I am Prince Charming."

"Prince Charming of what kingdom? Charming is a very common name these days," Arrow said.

Wen nodded. He knew three Charmings.

"Prince Charming of Whares." Charming lurched forward and grabbed Arrow's hand. "I'll protect you in this accursed place, fair maiden—"

"You can call me Arrow."

"—fair Arrow," Charming said without hesitation, "and see you safely through it if it's the last thing I do!"

Wen wasn't sure whether to laugh at Charming's demeanor or to feel indignant at his presumption that Arrow needed him. "I think Arrow is quite capable of seeing herself safely through this place," he said.

The prince barely glanced at him. "It is obvious," he said in a loud whisper, "that your companion is ill-equipped for such a forest."

Wen let his annoyance sweep over him. "Look who's talking. I'm not the one who got knocked out."

Arrow choked back something sounding suspiciously like a laugh.

"Just look at his shield; it's dented!" Charming said.

"You don't even have a shield," Wen said through gritted teeth, and then he wondered why he was bothering to get worked up over this idiot.

"My dear Prince Charming," Arrow said regally, "thank you for your offer of assistance, but I find I am quite enamored with my current companion."

"Enamored?" Charming's disbelieving gaze slid to Wen.

Wen raised his eyebrows at Arrow. She winked at him. "I'm sure if you're in the forest for long, you'll find someone who really needs your help, Prince Charming. While you search for this person, I would highly recommend not tangling with any trolls in the future, at least not without a weapon. Good day to you."

"But—but—" The prince tried to stand and then promptly sank back down. "Oh, my head is spinning."

"You'll be all right." Arrow patted him on the arm and straightened. "Just don't go to sleep until your dizziness has passed." She walked back toward Bay.

"I'll find you!" Charming cried, a hand pressed to his head. "I'll find you again, fair Arrow, fear not!"

With a quick, backward look at the spluttering Charming, Wen hurried after Arrow. He reattached his shield to the saddle and mounted. "Princes like that are what give the rest of us a bad name," he muttered.

"At least we know my damsel in distress disguise is working." Arrow tucked the water flask into a saddlebag.

"Except you were battling the troll and that was certainly not like a damsel in distress." Wen sighed. "Never mind. Come on. We should keep moving. There might be more trolls around here."

"Yes, for another five point six eight three kilometers, according to that troll crossing sign." Arrow took the hand Wen offered and sat sidesaddle in front of him once more. Bay took off at a gallop on the path, clearly desperate to get out of potential troll territory. Arrow held fast to Wen with one hand. "What?" she asked, when she noticed how Wen was looking at her.

"Five point...right."

"I'm serious." There was no trace of sarcasm in her voice.

"How could you possibly know how far we've traveled since the sign?" he asked.

Arrow shrugged. "I can always tell distances. Just like I know it was one point six three kilometers from the clearing where we woke up to Rumpel Stiltskin's house, and two point seven nine two kilometers from there to the troll crossing sign." She pushed his gaping jaw closed. "I'm good with numbers, all right? Numbers, and directions, and everything related to them."

She sounded serious, but he wasn't sure if she was pulling his leg. "All right, what's ninety-six multiplied by eighty-seven?"

"Eight thousand, three hundred fifty-two," she said instantly.

It took Wen a minute to figure that out, and only then by drawing imaginary numbers on his hand.

His amazement growing, he said, "One thousand, one hundred ninety-four divided by six."

"One hundred ninety-nine."

Another minute while he calculated that. "The square root of three hundred ninety."

"Nineteen point seven four eight four one seven six five eight one three one five."

He would take her word on that one. "You said directions too? What direction are we going?"

"At this moment, north-northeast. Guess how many times I've ever been lost?"

"Never?"

Arrow smiled.

"I'm very impressed," Wen said. "Anything else you're good at besides math and directions?"

"Science. History. Literature. I remember anything I read perfectly. Names, dates, stories, facts. I was so bored with school, I have to tell you. I used to get in trouble for falling asleep on my tutors."

"I'm very, *very* impressed."

"I have a good memory, that's all."

"That seems a little more than 'that's all.'"

Arrow turned her face away so he couldn't read her expression. "Right," she said softly.

He frowned at the back of her head, puzzled by her sudden glumness. Bay galloped onward, until at last Arrow said, "We're out of the troll crossing zone. It doesn't mean we won't see more, but maybe we'll be very lucky."

6 – Relentless Royalty

Bay slowed to a canter and then a steady walk. Wen continued to keep a sharp eye on the trees. He still occasionally thought he glimpsed things moving within the forest, but nothing attacked them. He paid close attention to the yellow flowers that blossomed along the path—some miniscule, some larger than his head—and steered clear of them, as recommended by Rumpel Stiltskin.

"We might stumble on an enchanted princess in here," Arrow said. "The chances are actually pretty high."

A sudden weight descended in Wen's stomach, as if he had swallowed a giant rock. "Yes."

Arrow tilted her head at him. "You sure don't sound pleased about it. Come on, you were worried about how you might find enchanted princesses in such a short amount of time, and almost immediately we end up in here!" She waved her hand at the forest.

"I know, I know. It's just…"

"Just?" Arrow prompted.

He could only meet her lively eyes for a moment before he looked at the ground. A frown puckered his forehead. "Hair."

"It's just hair?" Arrow asked in disbelief.

"No, look, hair." Wen brought Bay to a stop and got off the horse. Arrow slid into his waiting arms, and when he set her down, she followed him over to the hair on the path.

"Wow, I'd hate to have that much hair," Arrow said.

Wen's eyes followed the hair. It stretched across the path and into the forest on either side, glimmering a brilliant gold in the sunlight cast on it through the leaves.

48

Arrow bent down and studied it before touching it. "Hmm. I wonder which way the person attached to this is." She picked up a small handful of hair and pulled it toward her. It kept coming...and coming...and coming, until at last, the ends of the hair slithered onto the path. "Not to the right, then!"

"What if it's not attached to anyone?" Wen asked.

Arrow pulled the handful of hair the other direction. It came toward her, but only for a moment. It pulled taut and there was a high-pitched cry from somewhere off to their left. "Nope, it's definitely attached."

Wen had already started that way, following the tresses into the trees. "Bay, wait here!"

Bay neighed his agreement.

A short distance into the trees, they found the maiden with the ridiculously long hair. She sat on a log and wept into her hands. Her silky green dress was smudged with dirt and torn in several places. Her head jerked up at their footfalls and she gazed at them with wide, tragic, hazel eyes.

"Oh! I am saved!" The maiden clasped her hands together.

"Hello, there," Arrow said in a tone generally reserved for very young children. "What's your name?"

"Rapunzel." She looked around fourteen or fifteen. "Please, tell me, have you seen my love?"

"Your love wasn't a skinny man with black hair, was he?" Wen asked, thinking of the bird man.

"No, my love has locks of the lightest brown, and his eyes are like the richest of walnuts, and his face is as if carved from the purest marble!"

Marble. Right. "No, we definitely haven't seen him," Wen said.

Rapunzel burst into tears again. "I must find him!" she wailed. "I must! I was locked in that horrible tower for years, and then I finally met my true love and that evil, evil witch cut off all my hair and my love is missing, and what do I do?"

Wen latched onto one detail that didn't make much sense to him. "Your hair looks perfectly intact to me."

"It grew back!" Rapunzel choked out through sobs. "I drank from yonder spring and my hair was suddenly back,

49

and it has caught on so many trees!"

"I wonder if your hair was magicked to grow so long in the first place," Arrow mused, walking around Rapunzel. "Maybe there's a spring in here that re-enchants a previously broken spell. Oh, I'd love to get a sample of that water to bring home for testing. Do you know where it was?"

Rapunzel stared at Arrow. "What?"

"Never you mind, darling," Arrow said kindly. "You wouldn't happen to be a princess, would you?"

"Yes, yes, I am!"

"Do you *want* to lug around all that hair?" Arrow asked. "Do you think maybe you'd consider cutting off a hundred meters or so?"

"Anything that will help me get more quickly to my love! How can I look for him when I can't even walk through the forest?"

"That," Arrow said, "is the most sensible thing I have heard you say yet. Wenceslas, please cut off some of her hair."

Wen thought he saw where Arrow was going with this. He raised an eyebrow at her, and she gestured at Rapunzel's hair. "I could do it with my club, but the sword would probably be faster," she pointed out.

Wen drew his weapon and stepped closer to Rapunzel. Arrow gathered up Rapunzel's hair halfway between her hips and her knees and held it steady. Wen sliced through the hair, and as soon as he had cut the last silky strand, Arrow gasped and poked her fingers in her ears. "That pop was really loud."

"Pop?" Princess Rapunzel asked.

"The magic in here is so strong that it kind of pops and hurts my ears when it breaks. Your hair enchantment is broken now," Arrow said. "Again, apparently. Now, then, would you like to come with us?"

"One moment, please," Wen said to Rapunzel. He sheathed his sword and pulled Arrow aside. "Arrow," he said in a whisper, "please tell me that you're not trying to set me up with her."

"Tch, no. Wait a second, did you think I told you to break her enchantment so you could try to marry her and fulfill your giftcurse?"

"It crossed my mind."

Rapunzel burst into another round of loud tears behind them, and the only words Wen could make out were "my love" and "forever".

"Wenceslas, she's *weepy* and *in love with someone else*," Arrow said. "I told you that we would try to find you a girl you like and want to marry. Do you want to marry someone who's wailing away about her true love?"

"Not particularly."

"Well, then. Let's help her because it's the right thing to do and we don't want her to get eaten by a troll, shall we?"

Before Wen could agree, someone shouted, "Rapunzel! Rapunzel!"

Wen and Arrow turned as a young man with brown, curly hair burst through the trees. "Rapunzel!" He looked quite ordinary, certainly not like his face was carved from marble, pure or otherwise.

"My love!" Rapunzel shrieked. She flung herself on the young man and planted kisses all over his face.

"Oh, Rapunzel, I thought I would never find you!"

"Oh, my love! My love! What happened to you?"

He rattled off some story about being blind and then being healed by someone in the forest, and finally stumbling upon Rapunzel's hair and following it. When he was finished, he heard Rapunzel's rambling tale and thanked Arrow and Wen profusely.

"Please, take this as a token of my thanks." The young man pressed a golden acorn into Wen's hand. "If ever you should find yourself in need of aid, throw it into the air and call for Beeswax."

"Beeswax," Wen echoed in disbelief.

"Indeed, humble woodcutter!" the young man exclaimed.

Arrow grinned and hopped once, obviously pleased that her disguise for him had worked so well.

Wen tucked the golden acorn into his pocket. "Can we do anything to help you?"

"No, no, we'll be just fine," the young man said stoutly. "Fair travels to you both." He bowed with flourish, took Rapunzel's hand, and led her off into the trees, leaving her trail of cut hair behind.

Arrow looped her arm through Wen's. "We are doing

fantastically. Half a day in Tisi Forest, and we've helped break three enchantments! All right, technically, the switching spell wasn't really *us,* but if we hadn't distracted the troll, that awful man wouldn't have been able to switch with him, so that counts."

"I don't know about you, but all of these enchantments have made me hungry. Shall we go find Bay and get some food?"

"Yes, let's." Arrow shook his arm enthusiastically as they followed Rapunzel's hair back toward the path. "And then I want to see if we can find that spring Rapunzel was talking about and bottle some water from it. I tell you what, Wenceslas, I have a great feeling about being in this forest. I—"

"Fair Arrow!"

Wen and Arrow swung around as Prince Charming of Whares pushed through the trees. He now had a sword, though no scabbard, so he had nowhere to put it away. "We meet again! It must be destiny!"

"Oh, for the love of dragons," Arrow muttered. "Where did you get that sword?"

"I found it sticking out of a rock," Charming said promptly, "very near where you left me. As soon as I touched it, my head was suddenly clear and no longer ached! And then I said to myself, I said, 'Charming, you dashing fellow, now you should find fair Arrow again and she will see that you can protect her better than her blumbering companion.'"

Wen took a step forward, and Arrow flung out an arm to hold him back. He stopped and pointed a finger at Charming. "Blumbering isn't even a word." Out of the side of his mouth, he whispered, "How did he catch up to us? We've been riding on Bay."

"Magic forest," Arrow said. "And it seems he might have a magic sword. Perhaps it took him where he wanted to go."

Wen frowned. "To you?"

"I told you I would find you," Charming said. "Now that I have a magical sword, all will be well! I'll escort you out of this place, and then we'll be married—"

Arrow choked. "Excuse me, who said anything about marriage?"

52

"I did." Charming looked at her with great concern. "Didn't you hear me?"

"That was a rhetorical question," Arrow said.

"You should leave the rhetoric to the minstrels at the minstrel institution. I hear they're quite skilled at it," Charming said.

"What? No, not—oh, forget it. I'm not marrying you."

"Are you already betrothed?" Charming asked.

"No, but—"

"Then there's no trouble!" Charming swung his sword in a mock swordfight. "I shall protect you now and forever, I'll—"

Wen's hand went to his sword hilt; he was so close to drawing it and challenging the idiot prince to a duel just to get him to go away.

Arrow caught his motion and pressed her hand against his, silently warning him against drawing the weapon.

"Just let me poke him with the sword a little," Wen whispered.

"Magic sword, Wenceslas," she hissed. "What if it's an invincible sword or one that instantly kills anyone who attacks the bearer?"

"It might be worth it to try," he grumbled. Arrow pursed her lips at him, and he hastily added, "I'm kidding. Mostly."

Arrow shook her head. "You didn't ask whether I want your protection," she said to Charming.

Charming stared at her as though she were speaking a foreign language. "Of course you want my protection. I'm Prince Charming of Whares!"

"And I'm so not impressed. Find a girl who doesn't mind your hubris—"

Charming's forehead furrowed. "My hew breeze? What?"

Arrow sighed. "I'm done." She moved her hand off Wen's and turned to walk away.

"Wait! Fair Arrow!" Prince Charming leapt in front of her, blocking her path. "Don't you *want* a dashing prince to accompany you through this forest of magic?"

Arrow waved at Wen. "I already have a dashing prince accompanying me through this forest of magic."

Charming eyed Wen up and down. "But I'm more dashing than him!" he said, as though under some ridiculous notion that if he could prove himself more dashing, Arrow would swap princes.

Arrow looked between them. "Wenceslas is taller."

Charming and Wen sized each other up. She was right, though Wen was barely taller.

"Oh." Charming's shoulders sagged. "I see."

"Don't feel bad," Arrow said kindly. "I'm sure you'll find a damsel who doesn't mind your lack of height."

Wen suppressed a laugh. "This coming from the girl who barely reaches my chest," he whispered so that only she'd be able to hear.

Arrow nodded toward Charming, who was staring down at himself in a despondent sort of way. "He'll bounce back quickly once he finds some other trait to brag on. We'd better get out of here fast." She raised her voice. "Good day, Prince Charming of Whares."

"My fair Arrow! I'll—I'll find you!" Charming didn't sound nearly as assured as he had the first time he'd said this.

Wen and Arrow ignored him and hurried onward, once again following the trail of Rapunzel's hair.

"So you think I'm dashing, do you?" Wen asked.

"Of course you're dashing," Arrow said without any hint of bashfulness. "At least you don't flaunt it and think it makes you better than anyone else."

He grinned at her. "You mean I don't have hubris?"

"You win extra points for knowing that word."

"Well, when you..." Wen trailed off as he and Arrow reached the path. "Where's Bay?" He stared up and down the trail. "Did the hair move?"

"No, this is exactly where we left him." Arrow turned worriedly on the spot, her eyes sweeping over the trees. "Maybe he just wandered up the path a little way? Looking for something tasty to eat?"

"Bay!" Wen called, but there was no answering whinny, no clomping of hooves rushing toward him. "BAY!"

"We'll find him," Arrow said in determination.

"What if a troll got him? What if he ate a yellow flower and something happened to him?" Wen squeezed the hilt of his sword. Bay had been his only constant companion since his giftcurse had begun forcing him out of his castle.

"We'll *find* him, Wenceslas. Look!" She darted down the path, the way they had been heading when they found the hair, and pointed at the ground. "Hoof prints! Only a few, but I'll bet he went this way. Let's look, and if we can't find him in a short while, we'll figure out what to do next, all right?" She grabbed his hand and squeezed it, and he nodded.

They kept moving, occasionally finding a faint hoof print outlined in the dirt path. They passed a house on one side—well, half a house, really. It appeared to be made of gingerbread and was adorned with a lot of different kinds of candy, but it was partly eaten away.

Arrow paused to look at the remains of the gingerbread house. "It's not moldy or anything. I wouldn't eat it anyway, even as hungry as I am and as delicious as those giant chocolate bonbons on that door look..." She turned resolutely from the candy house and marched forward.

"Bay!" Wen called again. Still nothing.

The path cut through a huge, wide clearing full of grass and wildflowers. None that were yellow, Wen noticed in relief. Jutting up from the middle of the flowers was an enormous beanstalk.

Everyone knew that giants lived at the top of magic beanstalks, and Wen and Arrow debated the possibility that a giant had come down and carried Bay away with him. "I don't think a giant has been here recently. Look at the clearing—the flowers aren't crushed and there are no footprints." Arrow said.

"But a giant could have stayed on the beanstalk and snatched Bay from there," Wen replied.

They poked around the clearing a bit, in search of hoof prints, and found nothing, though underneath all the wildflowers, it was kind of hard to tell if something was there or not.

"Wenceslas, I would climb that beanstalk and face a giant if I thought Bay might be up there, but we just don't *know.*"

"I know," Wen said despairingly. His poor horse. "Something had to have happened to him, Arrow. He wouldn't wander away like this. He wouldn't."

Arrow walked along the path, searching the ground for

Bay's tracks. She was out of the clearing and among the trees once more, almost out of sight, when she called, "Wenceslas!" She held up her helmet. "He went this way."

7 – The Frog Princes

Wen ran over to Arrow and they hastened forward, Arrow shoving her helmet down on her head, which looked even odder with her dress than it had with her trousers. They stopped just as suddenly when, not far away from the clearing, the trees opened once more—this time, at the edge of a huge bog.

Bay stood near the bog, and touching his flank was an older woman. She looked at them and smiled—a smile that Wen wasn't sure he liked. Her face was smooth of wrinkles, even though her hair was gray. She laughed and Wen *definitely* didn't like it.

"Hello, my dears." Her mossy green eyes trailed over Wen, and a feeling like ants crawling over his skin made him shiver.

Rumpel Stiltskin's warning about going around a bog if they should happen upon one rang through Wen's mind. "Bay," he said urgently.

Bay didn't respond, didn't so much as turn toward Wen.

"What did you do to him?" Wen demanded.

"Oooh, a prince! I knew this horse belonged to a prince! I was sure of it!" The strange woman clapped her hands delightedly. "Charm the horse to charm the prince, yes?"

A wonderful, peaceful feeling swept over Wen, and he wanted very much to walk down and be with the woman, to go wherever she told him to and to spend forever and eternity and beyond with her.

As he made to step forward, Arrow's fingers slid in between his. He was only vaguely aware of it until a warm feeling spread from the place his palm touched hers and flooded through his body, and the fogginess on his mind lifted. He jerked back, breathing rapidly, his heart pounding. What had he been thinking?

Arrow was holding her club up in front of them like a shield. It glowed faintly, and her other hand still gripped Wen's. "You can't have him, witch," she said. "And you give that horse back at once!"

The witch next to Bay scowled ferociously. "Sorceress," she spat. "You won't steal this delicious prince from me."

Wen wasn't sure the witch meant that he *looked* delicious or would *taste* delicious and didn't want to find out either way.

"Don't let go of me," Arrow whispered. "I don't quite know how I'm doing this. Contact can help break charms, though."

He squeezed her hand. "I won't."

"No!" The witch stamped her foot, as if she were a child whom Arrow was depriving of sweets. "He'll make a fine addition to my collection, and I won't have some little sorceress take him!"

Wen wasn't entirely sure what happened next. There was a bright flash of light that blinded him, Arrow cried out, and her hand was torn from Wen's. The worst pins-and-needles sensation Wen had ever experienced covered his entire body, so painful that he wanted to scream, but his vocal cords didn't seem to be working. He felt *strange*, not like himself at all. His limbs weren't cooperating.

His vision slowly came back to him, and when it did, the whole world was wrong. The ground was right in front of his face—had he fallen?—and everything looked so much bigger than it should have. He tried to push himself up and then discovered what the problem was: He didn't have arms.

Wen stared at the appendages attached to him. He waved a webbed hand in front of his face. Webbed. Green. He was green again, and it wasn't because Arrow had turned his skin a different color. With a sinking horror, he realized what had happened.

He was a frog. A *frog.* The blasted witch had turned him into a frog!

"Oooh, how lovely! You're such a pretty shade of green!"

The witch's giant face loomed in front of him and massive hands came toward him. Wen tried to scramble away, but he wasn't used to a frog body and didn't know how to properly use his legs, and she scooped him up easily. "I've never yet met a prince who turned into such a bright green! You will be a fantastic addition! Oh, I love you already!"

Wen got a glimpse of Arrow, slumped against a tree, as if she had slammed backward into it. He didn't have time to see if she was breathing before the witch's hand closed down on top of him and covered him in darkness. He pushed against her hands, but to no avail, and she cackled delightedly as she carried him away...somewhere.

He couldn't even practice using his legs; he was held too firmly between her palms. He wasn't sure he could talk, either. He gave it a try, if only to hold back his panic at being a frog carried by a crazy witch.

"Hello."

His voice seemed to come from the depths of his stomach and out of his mouth. It sounded croaky and not at all like him, but he was speaking, so at least he had that.

Unless he was really croaking and it only sounded like speaking to his frog ears. Did frogs *have* ears? They had to, or he wouldn't be able to hear.

Calm down, Wen, calm down. There has to be a way out of this. There has to be.

Is Arrow all right? Did the witch kill her or just knock her unconscious? She has to be unconscious, right? She's Arrow. She couldn't just...she couldn't be...

It was several minutes before the witch released him, and even when she set him down, he was disoriented and it took a moment to figure out where he was.

He was in some sort of glass terrarium, like his fifth eldest brother had always used to keep lizards. Four walls of glass imprisoned him, and above him—high, high above him—the witch was busy fitting some sort of mesh over the top. Inside of his glass cage, there was a little pool of water and a patch of planted moss and grass.

"There you go, my lovely," the witch cooed. "That will be the perfect home for you."

"No," he said, adjusting more to talking with every word, "this will not be the perfect home for me. I insist you release me at once."

"That's what all my frog princes say. You'll come round in a year or two. You all be nice to our new prince, my lovelies." Chortling, she walked across a room and out a door.

Wen hopped awkwardly over to the side. He pressed his face as close to the glass as he could and was horrified to see that he was on a huge table crammed full of terrariums just like his, each with a frog in it. "Hello?" he called tentatively.

There was a chorus of despairing, "Hello," from the others.

"How'd she get you, then?" the frog in the terrarium directly beside him asked.

"She charmed my horse," Wen said glumly. "And then my friend, Arrow—" He stopped. He couldn't get the image of her unmoving body slumped against the tree out of his mind.

"What's your name, then?" his neighbor asked him.

"Wen. What's yours?"

"I'm Humphrey. Been here two months. At least, I think it's been two months. It's easy to lose track in here."

Wen eyed the mesh top. "Has *anyone* ever escaped?"

"Once Bartholomew got out, but he got caught by a fox and eaten. Gerald was the only one who really escaped, and he just got lucky," one of the other frogs said. "I'm Rathbert, by the way."

"How did Gerald get lucky?" Wen asked. Maybe he could find that sort of luck.

"Some princess stumbled in here while the witch was out. Gerald convinced her to kiss him—according to the witch, that's the only way to break our spell, a princess's kiss—and then he ran off with her. *Without* letting out the rest of us!" Rathbert called Gerald a very nasty name.

"Great," Wen grumbled. "Princesses again. Well, I'll have to find another way out. I'm not spending the rest of my life as a pet."

"Sorry, Wen," Humphrey said sympathetically. "There's no way out. You think we haven't tried everything possible?"

"There has to be a way." *Always a second option, Arrow? What's my second option here?* And this was followed by a quieter thought directed her way. *Please be all right.*

None of the other frog princes said anything, but Wen had the distinct impression they pitied him for his idealism.

The door opened again, and Wen fully expected to see the witch returning. Instead, it was Arrow who slipped through. An enormous bubble of worry popped, and relief swelled to take its place.

"Wenceslas? Are you here?" Arrow whispered. "I saw that mad witch leaving...she's tried to hide this place with magic, but I saw right through it. Stupid hag, who does she think she is, throwing me against a tree? She can't even knock a person out properly. *Wenceslas!*"

"Here!" Wen shouted, hoping he was really speaking and not just croaking.

Arrow turned toward the table of frogs. He couldn't see her face through her helmet. "You're a *frog?*"

"Yes!"

She came closer. "Which one are you?"

Before he could answer, all of the frogs hopped around in their terrariums, shouting, "Me! Me! Here I am!"

"Tch. You are not all Wenceslas." Arrow bent down to examine them, and right as Wen opened his mouth to tell her something that would prove his identity, she pointed at him. "You're my prince."

The other frogs protested mightily, and Arrow leaned toward Wenceslas and asked, "What did we encounter on our first night together?"

"A dragon," he answered promptly, "and a water nymph."

"Please! Please! Take us with you!" the other frog princes begged.

"I'm almost tempted not to, what with you trying to trick me into taking you instead of Wenceslas," she said to the lot of them. "But I wouldn't even leave lying princes to that horrible hag. Come on, then. Quickly, I don't know how long we have." She yanked the mesh off of Wen's cage and picked him up, depositing him carefully in her breast pocket. Then she pulled off her helmet, flipped it upside down, and grabbed the other frogs and dropped them into it. Some of them shouted out their eternal love and gratitude to Arrow, until she told them all to shut up.

Arrow was turning to leave when the door opened. Over

the edge of her pocket, Wen could see the witch standing in the doorway. The witch shrieked and dropped a basket she was holding, and vegetables rolled across the floor.

"*My princes!*" The witch raised her hand, enraged, and Arrow ducked as some kind of spell flew past her.

"Oh, no, you don't, you stupid, evil, prince-stealing witch!" Arrow shouted. She snatched her club from her side and swung it through the air. It glowed brightly, and a swarm of huge, flying bugs appeared and pelted straight into the witch.

Arrow threw herself to the side and something that looked like a flash of lightning shot past. The room resounded with the sound of shattering glass, and the witch screamed, "NO! My princes' beautiful homes! *You wretched sorceress! Die! Die now!*"

Arrow dove behind a couch and almost squished Wen with her arm. He fell all the way into the pocket and couldn't see anything that was happening. There was a tremendous crash and a sound like a howling wind, and then more crashes, so close and loud that Wen would have covered his ears had he known how to do so.

Then everything got very quiet. Wen pushed himself up with his back legs and struggled to see out of Arrow's pocket. He finally got his head over the edge and bright sunlight met his eyes.

The room they had been in was gone. In fact, whatever house or cottage the room had been in was gone. In a giant circle surrounding Arrow—Wen saw this because Arrow turned on the spot—there was nothing but piles of broken wood and bits of thatch here and there. Arrow was untouched in the middle of it, like the epicenter of a hurricane. The witch's legs stuck out from under one of the piles of wood, and Bay stood outside of the rubbish heap.

"Arrow," he said slowly, "did you just blow down the witch's house?"

"I think so?" Arrow's reply was more of a question than an answer. "I wasn't trying to! I just wanted a way out!"

The frog princes in Arrow's helmet cheered loudly.

Wen moved up and down slightly as Arrow walked cautiously over to the witch. She pushed aside the wood with her club to reveal the witch underneath, bearing a huge lump on her forehead.

"She's still breathing," Arrow said.

The frog princes groaned, and one of them—Wen thought it was Rathbert—shouted, "Kill her! Kill her now!"

"I'm not going to kill her," Arrow snapped.

"Then she'll just keep changing princes into frogs and locking them up," Rathbert said.

"Oh, no, she won't." Arrow aimed her club at the witch, and flowers burst out of the tip of it. She gave it a shake, grumbled something, and tried again.

There was a flash of light, and when Wen could see again, there was an ugly frog—he wasn't sure if he found it ugly as a human or a frog and decided it didn't matter—squatting in the place where the witch had been.

Wen's line of sight dropped and he almost fell back all the way into Arrow's pocket. It took him a moment to realize why: Arrow had sunk to her knees.

"Arrow?" He tried to see her face, but all he could see when he looked upward was her chin. "Are you all right?"

"Fine," she said, but her voice was wheezy. "That was a lot of magic. Just give me a moment."

"You did splendidly, my good lady!" Humphrey cried from the midst of the pile of frog princes. "Simply splendidly!"

The other princes chorused their agreement and called compliments over each other, as if to see who could flatter her the most and loudest.

Bay trotted over, picking through the rubble and looking absolutely enormous from Wen's perspective. He whickered questioningly, and Arrow reached up to pat his leg. "I'm fine, really." She stood to prove it, pulled herself up onto the saddle, and urged, "Hup, Bay!"

Bay was more than happy to pelt away from the witch's cottage and into the forest. Arrow peered down at her helmet full of frog princes. "Well, what am I supposed to do with the lot of you?"

"Are you a princess?" one of them asked eagerly.

"No, why?" Arrow asked suspiciously.

"According to the witch, a princess's kiss is the only way to break the spell," Wen explained. "Or so Rathbert said."

"Hm," Arrow mused. "Maybe it doesn't have to be a princess. Maybe any kiss would do."

Before Wen knew what she had planned, Arrow plucked him from her pocket and pressed a kiss to the top of his head.

Nothing happened.

Arrow dropped Wen back into her pocket. She pulled out her club and pointed it at the frogs in the helmet. "Hold still. I'm going to do a diagnostic spell to be sure."

Wen recalled Arrow saying she was good at diagnostic spells, and he was pretty sure she had used one on the enchanted bird, but he was rather glad that she wasn't aiming the club at him for once.

Light came out of Arrow's club and flooded over the princes. Arrow hummed and tucked the club away again. "Yes, you're quite right. Definitely a kiss from a princess spell. Blasted bat wings! Now I'm going to have to find a princess. Do you think Rapunzel already left the forest?"

"Can you not break the spell with your magic, my lady?" Humphrey asked. "That is to say, you did a marvelous job of turning the witch into a frog, so couldn't you do the opposite?"

"It might be possible if I have some time to study the enchantment, but in the meantime I could make things worse or I could end up a frog," Arrow explained. "Spells are supposed to come with an *out*. It's part of most magic—to create an enchantment, you have to have a way for the spell to be released or fulfilled. Sometimes that out *is* someone removing it with magic. And granted, for nasty spells, sometimes the release is death, but unless the witch told you that you have to die—"

"No, no, we saw it in action," Humphrey said hastily. "A princess kissed Gerald and he was a prince again."

"Then we should look for a princess while I study the enchantment. It's best and safest to use the out the witch created," Arrow said.

"Did you give her an out, then?" Wen asked curiously.

"Oh, yes. In order to turn back into a human, she has to get nine princes to kiss *her*." Arrow patted Bay's neck. "What do you think, Bay? Can we find a princess in this place?"

Bay whinnied determinedly.

"Right, then," Arrow said. "Onward!"

8 – Beeswax

Four days later, they had seen neither hide nor hair—long or short—of any princess.

"This is *ridiculous!*" Arrow exclaimed at the end of the fourth day. "We have faced trolls, witches, a crazy centaur, a horde of pixies, and seeing that idiot Prince Charming two more times, and we can't find *any* princesses?"

"On the bright side, I don't think Charming will be bothering you anymore, not after you turned his nose into a turnip," Wen said.

"He's just lucky I turned it back." Arrow slid off of Bay and set the helmet of tired frog princes on the ground near the small pond she'd found. The frog princes immediately hopped out of the helmet and headed for the water, and Arrow warned, "Do *not* go in that water until I test it, or who knows what enchantment could befall you?" She plucked Wen out of his now-usual spot in her pocket and set him carefully on the ground.

As soon as she'd studied the pond and declared it safe and unmagicked, Wen hopped toward it, anxious to wet his dry skin. He only took a quick dip and then hopped back to where Arrow was rummaging through the saddlebags.

"I'm behind you," he warned, so she wouldn't step on him.

Arrow looked down at the ground and then lay on her stomach so they were face-to-face. She set something in front of him. It took him a moment to recognize it, as it had been so much smaller from his perspective as a human, whereas now it was about half his size. It was the golden acorn that Rapunzel's true love had given him.

"I think we should consider using this. No matter how much I study that enchantment on you, I *cannot* untangle it. Obviously, the one time I tried didn't work very well."

"You did create a rather lovely flock of flamingoes," Wen said. "They would have looked much nicer if they hadn't tried to eat us, mind."

"Tch. None of you got eaten."

"Where did you get that?" He pointed his webbed toes at the acorn. "It was in my pocket."

"I have your clothes." Arrow paused. "Wait, did you think they transformed with you?"

"Well, that bird-man had his clothes when he changed back."

"Maybe the person who cast the bird switching spell put more care into it than the crazy frog witch."

"Fantastic, so I'll be naked if I get turned back?"

"Yes. Again. At least this time it won't be because you stood in front of a dragon and let it burn your clothes off."

"I did not *let* that dragon—" Wen stopped. "Never mind. If you really think that acorn can possibly help us break this spell, then yes, use it. I'm rather tired of eating bugs."

"Right, then." Arrow picked Wen up and stood. She set him on Bay's saddle, threw the acorn into the air, and shouted, "Beeswax!"

When the acorn hit the ground, there was a pop, a puff of smoke, and, coughing and waving the smoke from his face, a dwarf standing where the acorn had landed. He had pointy ears, a pointy hat, pointy shoes, and a pointy nose. In one hand, he held a spoon that dripped some sort of brown gravy, and he glared at Arrow from under bushy brown eyebrows. "Well! What kind of manners are yours then, interrupting a dwarf in the middle of his supper?"

Arrow curtsied and said, "I beg your forgiveness, good sir. My friend was told that if ever he was in need of aid, he could call on Beeswax."

"Aye, that's me," the dwarf said grumpily, though he seemed a little appeased by Arrow's apology. "Would've appreciated a house call not taking place during dinner." He paused and looked around. "Beg pardon, a forest call. Well, fine, now I'm here, we might as well get this over with. Where's your friend and what aid does he need?"

Arrow lifted Wen off the saddle and held him out toward Beeswax. "He's been turned into a frog and the only way to break the spell is to have a princess kiss him. I haven't been able to find any princesses."

Beeswax pulled a monocle out of his pocket and tucked it into his eye socket. He studied Wen and made "hmm" noises, and then nodded. "Yes, it appears to be a standard broken-with-a-princess's-kiss spell."

"That's what I just said," Arrow said, sounding mildly annoyed.

"Not sure I could break it even if I tried. It's kind of twisty."

"Yes, that's what I found too."

"So what do you want from me? Do I look like a princess to you?" He plucked the monocle from his eye and put it back in his pocket.

"Certainly not. You are the dwarfiest of dwarves I have ever seen," Arrow said, and Beeswax straightened up a little. "Perhaps you could tell us where we might find a princess? Or take me and the horse and my entourage of frog princes to a princess?"

"Good grief, there are more of them?" Beeswax looked around and spotted some of the princes at the edge of the pond.

Arrow placed Wen back on Bay's saddle. "Eight others besides him."

"Transporting *one* person would be a task, let alone a horse and nine frogs, and especially in this forest. Hard to navigate." Beeswax peered around. "Let me see what I can do about bringing a princess to you."

He disappeared with another pop and puff of smoke, and as soon as the frog princes got wind of what was happening, they all hopped over each other in their excitement to crowd around Arrow's feet and wait to see if they would be rescued.

Within five minutes, there was another pop and puff of smoke, and Beeswax returned with a young woman in tow. She had long, chestnut hair, a purple dress full of frills, lace, and jewels, and a bemused expression on her face.

"Here's your princess, then. Found her eating some gingerbread house elsewhere in the forest," Beeswax said.

"Now, if you'll excuse me, I'll be getting back to my dinner."

And then he was gone. The princess waved a hand in front of her face to blow away the smoke left behind. "Hello," she said to Arrow in bewilderment.

"Hello," Arrow said.

"Do you know where we are?" The princess looked around at the trees. "I was walking in my gardens and then suddenly, I was here! In a forest! I've been wandering all day."

"Yes, we're in Tisi Forest," Arrow replied.

The princess's face wrinkled in confusion. "Where?"

"It's a magic forest," Arrow said. "Chances are you're here so some hero or prince can rescue you and take you home. It happens quite a lot with princesses in Tisi Forest. Right now, though, I need you to help me out. My friend was turned into a frog, and I need you to kiss him, and then—"

The princess blanched. "A frog?" She took a step backward, and a cry went up from the ground. Her gaze fell upon the group of desperate frogs, and she screamed and turned to flee.

Arrow grabbed her arm and held her back. "Honestly, they're just frogs!"

The princess screamed again. Then again. And then she fell over in a dead faint.

"Stop it, all of you!" Arrow said sharply when the frog princes scrambled over each other to try to reach the princess's face. "You sit back and wait your turn, or so help me, I'll turn you into worse than a frog!"

They all fell back, except for Rathbert, who said, "Who are you to decide who gets kissed first?"

"I'm the one who saved you from that witch's house and carried you around in my helmet for four days, and protected you from that hawk, and checked all the water to make sure it wouldn't do anything to you!" Arrow snatched Wen off of Bay's saddle, bent down over the princess, and shook her shoulder. "Wake up, you silly girl."

The princess moaned and fluttered her eyelashes. She screamed and almost deafened Wen when Arrow shoved him in the princess's face. "Kiss him. Right now."

"*Eeeeeee!* I will not! Get it away, get it away from me!"

Arrow must have had a firm grip on the princess's arm, because try as she might, she couldn't scramble away.

"I don't have time for this! I want Wenceslas back!" If Arrow had been standing, Wen thought she probably would have stomped her foot. "How would you feel if one of your only friends got turned into a frog by a mad witch and you couldn't do anything about it?"

The princess's wide, terrified eyes were still fixed on Wen, but she seemed to calm down slightly at Arrow's question. "I suppose I would feel quite dreadful."

"Then please. Please, he'll be stuck as a frog unless I can get a princess to kiss him. Look, it doesn't hurt." Arrow kissed Wen on the head as she had days earlier. "See? I'm fine. It just doesn't work for me because I'm not a princess."

The princess made a whimpering "oooh" noise and shuddered. Tears filled her eyes and she took a deep breath. "I. Hate. Frogs."

"Then make the frogs go away. They're princes, all of them. Some of them have been trapped in their enchantment for years," Arrow said.

"For years?" the princess whispered.

"Years!" Rathbert exclaimed from nearby.

"Years," the princess echoed. There was a long silence. "I have eleven sisters...we..." She trailed off and swallowed. She looked between Wen and the other frogs. She whimpered again, squinched her eyes up, and gave Wen the tiniest peck of her lips on his head.

There was a flash of light, and the awful pins-and-needles sensation, and suddenly Wen was beside Arrow and the princess. He was on his hands and knees, which stuck out at angles, like he was getting ready to hop.

"Ohhhh!" The princess stared at him, her eyes wide, and Arrow immediately jumped in front of Wen, holding her arms out in an attempt to protect his nudity from the princess's gaze. "Oooh, you didn't say how handsome he is!" Her eyelids fluttered, but in an entirely different way than when she'd been coming out of her faint.

"Your clothes are in the saddlebags," Arrow hissed at him. "Get dressed, quickly!"

It took Wen a minute to readjust to having human fingers and legs, but he managed to find his clothing and quickly dress. He was sure he saw the princess trying to sneak glimpses of him as he hid behind Bay.

Bay chuffed and bumped Wen's shoulder with his nose, and Wen rubbed his flank. "I missed you too, boy."

"Are you willing to kiss these others now and turn them back into princes, too?" Arrow asked the princess.

"Yes, quite!" The princess had gone from looking disgusted to looking very anticipatory.

"Wait! Let me get something for them to wear." Arrow turned away from them all and pointed her club at the ground. It took her three tries, but she finally conjured eight sets of clothing.

"Eight men are going to be sorely missing their finery," Wen whispered in Arrow's ear.

She jumped, not having realized he had snuck up behind her, and smiled up at him. "I'm not used to you being back to your proper height yet. And," she added, nodding at the clothing, "judging by how rich all of those clothes look, the people who owned them can probably spare them. That's what I was aiming for, anyway."

The princess bent down and quickly kissed the frogs, one by one, and in brilliant flashes of light, they turned into naked men who scrambled to dress in the clothes Arrow had provided. Arrow turned her back on them, rubbing her ears and grimacing, no doubt experiencing the strong pops she felt when an enchantment broke in the forest. Wen cleared his throat and faced the same way. He wasn't sure whether or not the princess averted her gaze, but when the princes were fully dressed and Wen spun back around, the princess was avidly gazing around at the princes.

The ages of his fellow frog princes varied. The youngest looked to be about thirteen and the eldest had gray hair around a balding patch.

"My fair princess, thank you most kindly for breaking our spells!" A man a few years older than Wen dropped down in front of the princess and kissed her hand. He looked very clumsy as he did so—in fact, all of the frog princes looked very clumsy as they moved around. They had been frogs for much longer than Wen, and it showed in their jerky, awkward motions.

The princess giggled. "Please, call me Esme."

"Princess Esme, I am Prince Humphrey, heir to the throne of Lidoran. Will you allow me to escort you through this forest?"

"What? I wanted to escort her!" another of the princes said.

"I'll be escorting her, not you two idiots!" a third prince piped in.

"Back off, you scurvy knaves! I saw her first!"

"We all saw her at the same time!"

"Wenceslas?" Arrow murmured as the princes continued to squabble. "Do you want to stay and fight over Princess Esme and find out if she's enchanted? She seemed rather taken with you."

Wen, overwhelmed with gratitude that he wasn't a frog anymore, was busy getting a feel for his arms and legs again. "Hm? Oh, no, I don't want to fight eight princes for her." He wiggled his fingers, marveling at how beautifully unwebbed they were. "I don't know that I'd want to fight for her even if there weren't eight princes here."

"Why not?"

"I don't think she's my kind of princess."

"Well, I'm trying to help you narrow down your kind of princess, but the only thing I know so far is *not apathetic* and *not weepy and in love with someone else* and *not...*what is it about this one that's not right for you, aside from eight princes vying for her attention?" Arrow asked.

The princes were now shouting at each other, and Princess Esme looked to be thoroughly enjoying it.

"She was eating a gingerbread house in a magic forest, for one," Wen said.

"It was careless, you mean. All right, you want someone with common sense. I get it."

"She screamed when she saw a frog. She *fainted.*"

Arrow's lips twitched in a smile. "All right, you want someone—"

"You blew down a house for me," Wen said suddenly.

Arrow froze, looking flustered. "It was an accident."

"You carried me—and eight bickering princes—around for four days."

Arrow waved her hand. "Anyone would have done that."

"No, Arrow. They wouldn't have."

Arrow stared at him and her throat moved when she swallowed. She bent quickly to scoop her helmet off the ground and secured it to the saddlebag. She then stepped into one of Bay's stirrups to survey the princes.

"HEY! You unenchanted princes! It was nice knowing you. I wish you all the best in life. *Please* try not to get yourselves magicked before you get out of the forest again, all right? I believe Wenceslas and I will be departing now." She glanced at Wen, and he nodded his agreement. "Princess Esme, thank you for your help."

The princes paused in their arguing to say their good-byes to Arrow and Wen. They thanked Arrow profusely and proclaimed her charm and grace and beauty and kindness.

"All right, all right, enough!" She struggled to get away from them all.

Wen, already on Bay, reached down a hand. Arrow took it, and he pulled her out of the mass of princes and up in front of him. As Bay set off at a trot, Arrow smoothed her blue dress down and swiveled one foot idly in circles.

They didn't go very far; they were both very tired, and the sun was almost down. Once they were sure they'd got away from the princes, they set up their camp nestled among a ring of trees whose trunks glistened in the final rays of sunset. Wen tossed Arrow his blanket, and she caught it and began spreading it out.

Wen draped his cloak on the ground. "Did you mean what you said to Princess Esme back there?"

Arrow paused in her blanket-spreading and looked at him. "Everything I said was one hundred percent true. You should know that; we already talked about the downfalls of lying. But out of curiosity, to which part in particular were you referring?"

"The part where you told her I'm one of your only friends."

Arrow finished fixing the blanket and stood. "Yes. I— that is to say, my education didn't lend to making many friends. I have Penelope, but her father sent her away to her cousins' house three years ago, right after the giant chicken incident."

Wen wondered what her educational experience had been that it hadn't lent to making friends and what the giant chicken incident was, but Arrow's face was shadowed and he thought perhaps it would be better not to ask. Instead, he took two strides toward her and lifted her off the ground in a bone-crushing hug. She made an "eep!" of surprise.

"I'm glad to have a friend like you," Wen said. "Thank you for watching my back."

Arrow's arms slid around him. She patted his back and replied, her words half muffled by his shoulder, "I'm just glad you have a normal back to watch again."

Wen set her again on her feet. She was grinning at him, her melancholy wiped away, and an answering grin touched his lips.

He grabbed some of the remaining food out of his saddlebag—with only Arrow eating the past few days, it had lasted longer than it would have otherwise—and relished the taste of it. It was so good to get something in his stomach that wasn't squirming. Not that the bugs had tasted *bad* as a frog. They'd been delicious. The very thought of it made him feel rather nauseated now.

He swallowed a large bite of jerky and sat on his cloak. "Arrow, there's something I've been meaning to ask."

"Yes?"

"Back at the witch's place, how did you know which frog was me?"

Arrow's cheeks went slightly pink. Or maybe it was just the light from the sunset shining on her face. "Well, that was easy. When you were a frog, you were the exact same color as your eyes." She set her club within easy reach on the blanket.

"Arrow—"

"Sera."

Her voice was so quiet that he barely heard her. She met his eyes, very serious, and softly said, "My proper name is Serafina, but...Sera."

A smile spread across Wen's face. "Sera," he echoed. "Sera, is there *anything* you're afraid of?"

"Several things," she said lightly, "but I think we've shared quite enough tonight. Good night, Wenceslas."

"Good night...Sera."

9 – Sorceress of Nayrlanda

In the morning, Wen and Arrow—no, *Sera*—fed Bay and ate a small portion of their remaining food. "We're going to need to start picking berries or something," Sera said after they'd eaten. "Maybe we'll find a magic wishing rock and we can wish for a never-ending supply of food."

Wen finished packing up their belongings. "Maybe we'll be out of here before we need a magic wishing rock."

They mounted Bay and headed north-northeast, according to Arrow.

Sera.

Sera, Sera, Sera, Wen silently chanted.

"Hopefully if we keep going one direction, we'll find a path we can follow," Sera said.

Bay plodded through some underbrush and past a silvery elm tree, and Wen brought Bay to a stop.

"Well, would you look at that!" Sera bounced once. "Not a stone's throw from our camp! Except it might not have been here last night. I guess the forest decided it's done with us. At least it was kind enough to spit us out next to Nayrlanda."

Spread out before them was a huge city. Buildings covered the area as far as he could see, all over a sloping hillside. Towers and spires poked out of some of the buildings. Horses, carriages, and people entered and exited by way of a wide road that passed through gates and twisted up to the very top of the hill, where a citadel with golden spires and roofs presided over Nayrlanda.

Two gold statues stood on either side of the city gates. One was a woman holding an outstretched wand, the other a man with a heavy tome held out so that it almost touched the woman's wand tip.

Wen glanced over his shoulder. Tisi Forest was gone, as if it had never existed at all. The only thing behind him was the field in which they stood and some farmhouses in the distance.

"Hup, Bay," Wen said.

"Wait, wait!" Sera protested, and Bay jerked to a halt. "I have to change. Hang on."

Sera slid off of Bay on one side and rummaged in her bag. Wen jumped off on the other side and leaned against Bay, his eyes on the travelers entering and leaving the city.

"All right," Sera said after some rustling and clanking. She walked around Bay, dressed exactly as she had been the night Wen had met her: trousers, breastplate, and helmet.

"My turn," Wen said. It would probably be best to get into some clean clothes now that he no longer had to look the part of the humble woodcutter.

Sera turned while he changed. "Here's the plan: We'll sneak into Nayrlanda University, get into the records room, and gather up all the recent reports on enchanted princesses. Then we'll go looking for them. We still have about two weeks until your birthday. Twelve days, thirteen hours, and fifty-six minutes, if we're going to be precise."

"Oh. Right." With everything that had happened in Tisi Forest, Wen hadn't really been thinking about the plan to use Nayrlanda University to find enchanted princesses. A familiar lump of glum resignation settled into his stomach. "I'm ready."

Sera pushed her visor down, hiding her face. "Me, too."

She swung up behind Wen on Bay's saddle, and Wen nudged Bay down toward the road. They soon joined the throng of merchants and visitors. He recognized a group of seven dwarves who stood by the side of the road, pointing at a large map on the ground and arguing with each other. A flying carpet passed overhead, casting a shadow across them. A little girl in a bright red coat and hood pulled a muzzled, tied wolf on a sled toward the city gates.

There were also people who seemed to be suffering from enchantments. There was a woman whose legs appeared to have melded together, hopping along with the assistance of a boy. There was a massive talking dog, three mice trying not to get stepped on, and a swan chatting with a young man, who held the swan gently under his arm, and those were just a few of the faces among the crowd.

Wen and Sera soon passed the massive golden statues, imposing guardians of magic and knowledge.

"I always hated those statues," Sera muttered. "It's like they're there to tell you if you're not as good as they are at magic and knowledge, you're better off somewhere else. I turned them pink once."

"Pink?" Wen echoed.

"Yes, and covered in flower wreaths. I was eight. My father was not pleased."

"Did you visit Nayrlanda when you were young or did you live here?" Wen asked.

"I grew up here."

Wen waited to see if she would expand upon that, but she didn't. They maneuvered up the long, winding road toward the citadel on top of the hill—Nayrlanda University, which Wen had seen from a distance once before but had never visited. The city was bustling and full of people and creatures and street vendors selling merchandise. There were shops for bakers, butchers, dressmakers, magical wares, metalworking, apothecaries, glassblowers, weapons and armor, shoes, and anything else anyone could possibly want or need. The scent of horses mingled with the smells of all kinds of food and the tang of hot metal.

"I need to visit a blacksmith while we're here and get my shield repaired," Wen said.

"I know the best blacksmith here. We can go see her after we sneak into the university," Sera replied. "Ooh, but stop here, I want to get some more breakfast."

She leapt off of Bay before Wen could bring him completely to a stop and ran over to a vendor selling huge, sugar-coated pastries. By the time Wen had dismounted and walked Bay over, Sera had purchased two of them. She handed one to Wen. "Here you go, darling. In celebration of making it out of Tisi Forest in one piece."

"Thank you." The pastry was thick and soft, and it warmed Wen down to his toes. It was the best food he'd eaten in days. Sera ate surreptitiously, lifting her visor just enough to shove bits of pastry into her mouth.

It was about an hour before they reached the university on top of the hill. It was even bigger and more impressive up close. It wasn't just one building, but a group of buildings connected to each other by bridges or tunnels with glass windows. A low wall surrounded it, with gilded golden gates leading onto the grounds. It wasn't nearly as busy as the city's main gates, but there were people moving in and out. Some looked very scholarly, with armfuls of books. Others looked to be enchanted people or creatures seeking aid.

"All right, Bay, there are nice troughs of water and food over there for visiting horses." Sera pointed. "Could you please wait there for us until we're done here?"

Bay whickered and trotted over to the trough as if to prove how cooperative he was going to be.

"He'll be fine," Sera assured. "I promise," she added when Wen hesitated. "No crazy witch is going to run off with him and turn you into a frog again. We're going to sneak in through one of the side entrances. Come on."

The side entrance turned out to be a loose window in a secluded corner of one of the buildings. It led into a room full of dusty gadgets. Some were piled high around the room, and others were laid out on rows of shelves. Wen accidentally bumped into a twisted contraption that looked like a teapot melted onto something with metal tentacles, and it started screaming at him.

"Wenceslas!" Sera hissed.

"It was an accident!" Wen could barely hear himself over the noise of the shrieking teapot octopus thing.

Sera yanked out her club and pointed it at the teapot apparatus. It only got louder. Then she slammed her club into it, half crushing it, and it let out a feeble whine before falling silent.

Sera's head tilted up toward him, and though her visor was down, he was almost sure she was glaring at him. "Don't. Touch. Anything."

"I wasn't *trying* to! What is all this stuff?"

"Things confiscated from students, or magical experiments or lessons gone awry." Sera opened a door on the far side of the room, poked her head out, and waved Wen over. "If anyone asks," she murmured as he followed her out of the gadget room and into a brightly lit hallway, "Perseus sent us down here."

"All right." The lights in the hallway weren't torches, nor were they actually attached to anything. They were simply bright, hovering balls of light, evenly spaced along the walls near the ceiling.

Sera led them quickly and expertly through the building, ducking into rooms and yanking Wen after her whenever they heard anyone coming. "We're almost to the records room," she whispered the third time she'd hidden them from someone. She fingered her club. "Maybe if I put a sleeping spell on the clerk?"

Wen raised his eyebrows.

"Oh, please," Sera said, "he or she would probably thank me. Records is the most boring room in the history of ever."

"Wouldn't it be easier if I just walked into the records room and asked to view the most recent...?" Wen trailed off because Sera was already shaking her head.

"People aren't just allowed to peruse the records room unless they go to school here, and even then they usually have to get special permission from the professors. You'd have to explain who you were, and then you'd have to fill out a request to see records and tell *why* you want to see them. Trust me, a sleeping spell is easier."

Wen wondered what Sera would accidentally inflict on the poor clerk before she managed the sleeping spell, but he decided that unless he wanted her trying it out on *him,* he'd better keep his mouth shut about it.

"We're here. It's the room right around this corner." Sera poked her head out, looked around, and then grabbed Wen's arm and yanked him forward. There was a door with a sign on it that read:

RECORDS ROOM
Enter at Your Own Risk
Beware of the Dragon
Also, the Gremlins
Also, Also, the Monkey

Wen came to a dead stop and Sera looked over her shoulder at him. "Wenceslas, come *on*."

"Dragon?" He pointed at the sign. "Gremlins? Arro— Sera, I left my shield with Bay!"

Sera waved a dismissive hand. "Belly is an enchanted dragon; she's tame as anything. The gremlins are a bit of a pain if you don't know how to deal with them, but after two months in there, I know exactly how to handle them. It's the monkey you've got to watch for. It'll be fine, really." She opened the door to the records room, jumped in, and shouted, "HA!" at whoever was inside.

Wen followed after her apprehensively and walked into a cloud of grasshoppers flying around. He waved them out of his face. Sera held her club pointed at an astonished young man, who stood up from behind a desk. Behind him were rows and rows of filing cabinets and shelves stuffed with books and papers. The grasshoppers, Wen presumed, were the product of Sera's first attempt at the sleeping spell.

"Sera?" the surprised clerk asked.

"I'm Arrow!" Sera waved her club at him again, and several voles fell out of it and plopped onto the ground.

The young man behind the desk crossed his arms. "You've got Sera's club, *and* her voice, and—"

He stopped talking when Sera finally did a proper sleeping spell and he crumpled to the ground, snoring heavily.

Wen jumped backward and drew his sword when a vibrant red dragon, no bigger than a medium-sized dog, darted out from among the shelves and gobbled up several grasshoppers. It then pounced on one of the voles and swallowed it in one gulp. The other two voles scurried off and disappeared.

"Belly!" Sera dropped to her knees. The dragon pelted over to her and made a noise that sounded like bells chiming. "Have you been a good girl? I'm sure you have. I've missed you too."

Belly sat back on her haunches and gave a tiny roar that had a musical quality to it. Instead of breathing fire, a chunk of ice fell out of her mouth.

"Is she a baby dragon?" Wen asked curiously, crouching

down near Sera.

"No, she's full grown. She's got a spell on her that made her miniature and kind of different in general. Long story. Isn't she sweet? Belly, this is Wenceslas. He's a prince."

Belly hissed at him.

"No, Belly, he's a smart prince with a good head on his shoulders." Sera scratched behind Belly's ears and inclined her head toward Wen. "You'll have to forgive her; she's had some bad experiences with princes here in the records room." She gave the dragon one final pat and stood. "Go find the other voles, will you, Belly? I'd hate for them to start mating in here."

Belly chirruped and darted off into the shelves.

"All right, enchanted princesses..." Sera walked over to the desk and pushed the visor of her helmet up. She brushed a grasshopper off the desk and sorted through neat piles of paper in trays, grabbing a few sheets here and there. She turned to a filing cabinet nearby and pulled out several files.

Something jumped on top of Wen's head. He spun around and grabbed at it, but it screeched horribly at him and pulled on his hair so hard his eyes watered. He latched on to something warm and furry and tugged, but it clung to his hair even harder, and then started slapping him in the face and poking him in the eyes. When he finally wrenched it from his head, his eyes were sore and watery and he couldn't even see what he was holding, except that it was shrieking, squirming, and hitting his hands and wrists.

And then it bit him, and he dropped it. He heard sounds of scurrying, and he spun around, blinking and squinting.

"He's gone for now." Sera's face came into focus in front of him. "Oh, he got you good, didn't he?" She took his hand and examined the deep bite on his wrist. Blood dripped onto the smooth marble floor.

"Was that...?"

"I told you it was the monkey you had to watch for. He stops coming after you when he gets used to you. For the most part." Sera pointed her club at the ground. It sprouted flowers. She gave the club a shake, and a length of bandage appeared.

"Why doesn't the university get rid of him?" Wen kept a

80

sharp eye out for the monkey as Sera wrapped his bite with the bandage.

"They've tried," Sera said. "The monkey's magicked to be here by a fairy godmother spell. No matter how many times he's been moved or locked up, he always reappears in the records room, and no one can undo the magic. There are lots of theories as to why someone would use fairy godmother magic on a monkey to keep him here. I think that some fairy godmother got really mad at Nayrlanda University and stuck him here because he's so mean. You should see some of the hate magic that comes here."

Sera shoved the papers and files into Wen's arms. "Hold this. I think we've got enough, but let me check one more thing."

He trailed after her as she went down one of the rows of files and shelves. She stopped and pulled open a cabinet that read "P" with "Paupers – Princesses" beside it. She slid open the drawer and rifled through the files. A long, gray hand suddenly shot out from among the files and grabbed Sera's wrist with thin, spindly fingers. The grimacing face of a gremlin popped out of the drawer and half squealed, half growled, "Mine!"

"It is not." Sera snatched up a file and smacked the gremlin in the face. It let her go and rubbed its nose, scowling even more fiercely. "All right, we're set. Let's go." She dropped the file on top of the stack in Wen's hands and shut the drawer with the gremlin still in it.

"I thought you said the records room was boring," Wen said as Sera pushed her visor back down.

Sera opened the door and peeked out. "It *is*. It's all 'file this' and 'sort through that' and 'write up this report' and 'fend off the monkey until he gets bored with you' and 'interview these bespelled people and record what happened to them' and ughhh." She looked behind her as Belly darted out and bumped into the back of her legs. "Not now, Belly." She scratched the dragon's head. "I have to go. I'll come back sometime and bring you a nice rat, all right? Come on, Wenceslas."

They left the flowers sprouting from the floor and the clerk snoring behind the desk. They had barely started down the hall when a disbelieving voice from behind them

81

brought Sera to a halt.

"*Serafina?*"

Sera turned slowly, her shoulders hunching so that she looked even tinier than usual, and Wen turned with her. A woman stood there holding several files. She was very round and had a lot of laugh lines next to her eyes, though she currently looked quite stern.

Sera pushed her visor up. "Hello, Professor Haller," she said in a would-be brave tone.

"Serafina, I *hope* that you have just come from speaking with your father, but then I have to ask myself why you're all the way down here trying to hide your face with that ridiculous helmet."

Sera shifted her feet.

"I'll take that as a sign that you haven't seen your father," Professor Haller continued. "He's very concerned, and I'm sure he would be even more so if he saw you like this, and with—who is this?" She looked at Wen.

"Wen," Wen said, before Sera could deliberately butcher his name. He had contemplated using his full name and title, but given how these people viewed princes, he thought better of it.

"Tch," Sera scoffed. "My father isn't concerned about me. He's probably just angry I didn't come back after my last apprenticeship—"

"Yes, your last apprenticeship," Professor Haller interrupted. "Sorceress Lillian had quite a few things to say about that."

"I'll bet she did," Sera muttered. "Look, Professor Haller, I'm just here to help him." She jerked her thumb toward Wen. "And now I've got what I needed, so I'll be going."

"Serafina, your family—"

"—is probably a lot happier now that I'm not bothering them here," Sera finished.

"Serafina Nayrlanda, that is *not* true, and if you leave without speaking to your father, he will be most disappointed."

Nayrlanda. Serafina Nayrlanda.

Wen stared at Sera, dumbfounded. The Nayrlanda family had founded this school generations ago, built the city from the ground up, and were some of the most powerful and renowned sorcerers and sorceresses in the world.

Sera's face was pink with frustration. "Well, then, that won't be anything new for him!" She spun around and bolted down the hallway.

Professor Haller's expression was upset and saddened. Wen gave her a quick bow, said, "Nice to meet you!" and tore off after Sera, still clutching the papers from the records room.

10 – Seer's Prediction

Wen followed Sera the same way they'd come in, back through hallways and into the dusty gadget room. She pulled herself through the window before he'd even crossed the room, and by the time he was outside, she was disappearing around the corner.

She was quick, but his longer legs made him faster. He caught up to her at the front of the school. "Sera!"

She waved him off and continued her rapid pace toward the university's gates. Wen looked around for Bay. He was meandering around the food and water troughs with several other horses.

Wen whistled, and Bay's head jerked toward him. "Bay!" His horse trotted over to him. Wen paused to put the files and papers in one of the saddlebags, and by the time he did, Sera had gone through the front gates.

"Come on, Bay!" Wen grabbed Bay's reins and hurried out the gates, pushing through people coming and going. He spotted the shining silver of Sera's helmet bobbing among a crowd of women in fancy dresses. She turned a corner off of the main street.

Wen rounded the same corner and came to a halt. A pile of crates was stacked along the side of a dressmaker's shop, and Sera was seated on one of the crates. She didn't look over at Wen's footsteps or the *clop, clop* of Bay's hooves.

Wen dropped Bay's reins and sat on the crate beside Sera. Bay whinnied questioningly and chuffed against Sera's helmet.

Sera brushed her hand across Bay's nose. She lifted the helmet off her head and her pale red hair fell messily around her shoulders. She turned the helmet in circles in her hands and finally spoke. "My father's the headmaster of the university, but I guess you figured that out already. This place, this city—" She set her helmet beside her and turned her face toward the main street. "It's supposed to be my birthright. Every Nayrlanda since my great-great-great-grandparents has been super talented. Amazing sorcerers and sorceresses and all."

Wen nodded. He'd heard many stories of the incredible feats of magic produced by the Nayrlanda family.

"My brother Algernon was top of his classes at university. Now he travels around, breaking enchantments that baffle most sorcerers. Delphina wanted a family more than anything, but even she's the best healing sorceress you'll ever meet. Reginald has been performing perfect spells since he was two, and Elisabette is already starting basic classes at the university and mastering them all."

Wen put a hand on her shoulder. "You're not *them,* Sera."

"You don't understand," she said impatiently.

"Try me." The last time he had said that, she had averted the conversation with biscuits. He hoped she wouldn't avoid him now.

Sera's eyes closed. She seemed to struggle with herself, and then she said, "Years and years ago, right before my parents' wedding, the most well-known seer of the time told them that their third child would be the most brilliant sorceress the world had ever seen." Her eyes opened and a bitter smile twisted her lips. "From the day I was born, Mother and Father expected me to be...better. More than anyone else. By the time I was six, they still weren't even sure I could *do* magic. They did all sorts of things to test me. My mad aunt even thought it would be a good idea to tie me up and throw me in a pond, sure that my magic would surface and I'd float. Didn't bother telling my parents about her brilliant idea. It's a good thing Algernon was passing by when my aunt threw me in, or I'd have drowned."

"You think I don't understand?" Wen shook his head. "I'm an unmagical seventh son of a seventh son, remember? I told you they did all sorts of tests to see if I could do magic.

85

I never got thrown into a pond, mind, but my fourth eldest brother *did* almost set me on fire to see if I'd be immune to it. Mum stopped him just in time. People expected me to be all sorts of things I wasn't."

"It wasn't until I found this magic-enhancing club when I was eight that I was able to do any magic." Sera ran her hand over the club's sheath. "Even the university didn't want me. My own family's school...the professors all despaired of me. Told my parents I couldn't do anything right, and maybe I just needed some specialized training. So Father shipped me off to a sorcerer he knew, and the sorcerer sent me away when I accidentally set his tower on fire. Then they tried a wizard, thinking perhaps a different take on magic might make it stick with me. Mother and Father had a huge argument about it—Mother was reluctant to let me learn from a wizard instead of a sorcerer, but off I went! After a month, he told my father that even a rock could do better than me. Sorceress Lillian was my last one. She was horrible, Wenceslas—she made the strictest professors look as cute and cuddly as Belly. I ran away. I decided if I was going to do magic, I would do it on *my* terms."

"That's why you've been hunting for enchantments to break?" Wen asked softly.

"I figured if I could get out on my own and practice, I could show them all. Especially if I found some really im-pressive enchantments to break—like the sleeping spell tied up in that dragon you slew. That's why...that's why I'm Arrow. Because if I'm Arrow, it's all right if I can't do it perfectly. Arrow might not be a brilliant sorceress. Serafina is supposed to be."

Wen tilted his head to the side. Sera stared at her hands in her lap. "You're still the same person. Arrow or Serafina, you're always you."

Sera's fingers twitched. "I feel freer as Arrow."

"You told me your real name," he pointed out.

"Yes." She looked at him and a wistful smile crossed her face. "For the first time in a long time, you made me want to be Serafina again."

Sera pushed herself off the crate. Her head was level with Wen's as she stood in front of him. "My father's probably going to send people looking for me in the city any moment now."

"Seeing him couldn't be worse than a water nymph or a crazy frog-obsessed witch or that centaur you fought off in the forest, could it? Or Prince Charming?"

Sera groaned. "Oh, Wenceslas, are you kidding? I would take a frog-obsessed water nymph riding that centaur with Prince Charming over my father. I haven't done anything to prove that I'm even a smidge competent in my magic. My father would reprimand me and tell me how many mistakes I've made recently. He'd probably lock me up at home and refuse to let me do anything to help you. He'd tell you to go report your enchantment to the university so that one of their specialists could look into it. No. I'm not going to see my father, not now. Not until I finish what I've started."

Wen tapped the back of Sera's hand as she shifted anxiously from foot to foot, and she stilled. "My mum once told me something when my giftcurse was forcing me out of the castle again. She told me if I had to run, I should find something to run *toward*. For me, that's been running toward any enchanted princess I could find so I could eventually stop running. But I think maybe I was running away from what I really wanted. You convinced me I don't have to settle just to make this go away. So, Sera, are you running toward something, or are you running away?"

Sera's shoulders sagged. "What do I have to run toward, Wenceslas?"

"You made me a deal that you'd help me break my giftcurse one way or another," he said. "Now I'll make you a deal. Whatever *you* decide is worth running toward—I'll help you find it." He stuck out his hand. "Deal?"

Sera stared at his hand, then grasped it and shook it. "Deal." She tugged him forward and pressed a kiss to his cheek. "Thanks, Wen," she murmured.

He was sure he was blushing—his face certainly felt hot. "That's the first time you've called me Wen."

"I like Wenceslas. It fits you."

She dropped back down beside him and they sat in silence. She smoothed her shirt and fiddled with the hem of it, then suddenly clapped her hands together once. "Well, let's have a look at those enchanted princess files we got."

Wen retrieved the papers from his saddlebag and they

sat there in the alley, perusing the reports and deciding which ones seemed attainable in the two weeks he had left before his seventeenth birthday.

"Oh, look, here's a princess under a sleeping enchantment in a castle." Sera tapped a paper. "In Telsa. Not far from here. And the report says this isn't a spell that was set up between two kingdoms so the prince could rescue her. Let's see...thorns surrounding the castle, that's pretty standard. No mention of a dragon. Spell broken with a kiss, and it doesn't even say true love's kiss—just a kiss! And— yes, it lists her age. She's seventeen. This one looks great."

"Here's another one. This princess is locked in a tower." Wen scanned the paper. "Oh, never mind, it's a prince who put in a call for her rescue. And...oh, it was Rapunzel! I guess the university didn't need to worry about this one anyway."

"Oh! Oh, oh, oh, I've found a winner, Wenceslas! The king of Quells reported this. He has *twelve* daughters and he believes all of them to be under some sort of enchantment. Oh!" She looked at Wen with wide eyes. "Esme!"

He'd had the same thought. The princess who had kissed him out of his frog enchantment had said she had eleven sisters. "Maybe that's why she was willing to help us. Because she knows what it's like to be under a spell."

"This says the king's daughters are locked in a room every night, but in the morning, they're exhausted and their dancing shoes are all worn out." She waved the paper at him. "Twelve princesses. Aside from Esme, you might find you like one of them, right? The king is offering one of them in marriage to the person who can solve where they go every night."

They found a handful of others that seemed promising, and then Sera said, "All right, Telsa is closest, with the princess under the sleeping spell. We'll go there first, and if that fails, Quells is only a short distance from there. I don't know if we'll still have time after that, but if we do and you haven't found a suitable princess, we'll review the remaining reports that looked like they might work."

"We should probably see about getting you a horse before we go. Not that I mind sharing Bay," Wen said hastily, "but you might find it more comfortable having a horse of your own."

"Any money I have for a horse is at my family's house, locked away in a chest in my room. Actually..." Sera tapped her helmet. "I've got a few things stashed in my chest that might come in handy for us. Mother wouldn't let me bring any of it with me on my apprenticeships." She eyed Wen thoughtfully. "How do you feel about a quick side trip?"

***

Wen stopped with Sera in front of a beautifully wrought golden gate, behind which was a path made of pure white stones that led through intricate gardens up to a house on a hill. The house was the size of a small castle and had several towers, one of which had a round glass roof.

"Are you sure about this?" he asked.

"I'm always sure," Sera said confidently. "Almost always. Mostly. Some of the time. Anyway, yes, I'm sure about this. I doubt my family's home. Mother's probably off at some committee. Algernon and Delphina don't live here, and Reginald and Elisabette will be at the university with my father."

Wen glanced back the way they'd come. They'd left Bay at a stable in town and walked here. Sera had said trying to sneak a horse onto her family's estate would be far more difficult than trying to sneak the two of them.

Sera held out her hand toward the lock on the gate and murmured something under her breath. The lock clicked and the gate swung open, and Sera grabbed Wen's hand and quickly tugged him through it and off to the gardens on the side. "Our butler will have heard the gate open, come on!"

They stepped through colorful, flowering bushes and plants. A few garden faeries flittered here and there among the flowers, and two tiny female faeries sat on a lilac bush, chatting with each other. One of them saw Sera, made a squeak loud enough for Wen to hear, and grabbed her friend's arm. They zipped off into the branches in the time it took Wen to blink.

Wen and Sera went around some stables and the stable boy working there, creeping around to the side of the house that had the glass-domed tower.

"We can get in through one of the guest rooms. It won't set off any alarms; the house knows me," Sera whispered. "I'd go straight into my room, but there are no windows from my room that open on the ground floor. Mother and Father closed them all off after the incident with the murderous bushes." She looked around from the cover of a blossoming cherry tree and darted across the remainder of the lawn to the house, dragging Wen with her, cherry blossoms drifting around them.

Sera pressed her hands against a window and talked to it so softly he couldn't hear the words, and the window popped open. Sera, smirking at Wen, climbed through it. "The house always liked me. Come on in."

Wen was halfway through the window when it closed on his legs. He was pinned, unable to move either forward or backward.

It took Sera at least two minutes to convince the window that it wanted to let him go, that he wasn't a thief but a friend and that she would be very upset if it kept hold of him. The whole time, Wen waited for someone to walk by and see his legs sticking out the window, but no one came to investigate.

Finally, with what seemed like great reluctance, the window opened just enough to allow him to pull his legs into the house. Then it snapped shut and he was sure if it'd had a tongue, it would have blown a raspberry at him.

"Sorry about that," Sera said. "Apparently it doesn't like you very much. It's trained to recognize princes, though, so that might have something to do with it."

They stood in a bedroom of white stone walls covered in beautiful tapestries and decorations of gorgeous spun glass or intricate twisted gold. The bedposts were made of gold and topped with designs. Everything was impeccable. It reminded Wen a little of his castle, except somehow, the white walls of his home seemed a lot friendlier than the white walls here.

Sera poked her head out of the room and motioned Wen to follow. They entered a long hallway with portraits on the wall. The people were portrayed singularly and in groups, some of them holding wands, one with a giant feral cat, another with fingers covered in glowing jewels. Some bore a similarity to Sera, which made him think that he was walking through paintings of past Nayrlandas.

Dominating the wall at the end of the hallway was a huge painting of a family. A man with dark hair and Sera's blue eyes stood stiffly beside a woman who was the spitting image of Sera, save for her brown eyes. Posing around them were five children, three girls and two boys. Sera's family. Only Sera and the younger brother, Reginald, had red hair. The rest were all as dark-haired as their father.

Wen's eyes fell on the portrait of Sera. It looked like it had been done a few years earlier. The painted smile on her face was flat and didn't reach her eyes. She looked unhappy.

"Psst! Wenceslas!"

Sera had turned into a doorway but stopped when she realized Wen wasn't following her. She walked back over to him.

"I hated standing for that," she said. "Trying to be perfect. The perfect part of the perfect family." She scoffed. "That, and the painter kept shifting Reginald around to stand in front of Delphina because she was massively huge with her second child and he didn't want to paint that, as if it were something shameful. I wanted to hit him."

Sera moved away, and Wen took one last look at younger Sera's painted face before going after her into the tower with the glass dome. At the base of the tower was a room with a huge bed, sheer blue curtains around it, and simple wooden posts for the frame. One entire wall was filled with shelves holding books of every size, shape, and color imaginable. A large, sturdy desk and chair sat opposite of the shelves, and a wardrobe stood near the bed.

The room was full of all sorts of gadgets, and rolls of parchment were tucked into other spaces. It reminded Wen a little bit of the room full of confiscated and failed magical experiments at the university. A set of stairs began near the desk and twisted upward along the tower wall, up to a platform holding the biggest telescope Wen had ever seen. A cat lay on the bed, purring so loudly he could hear it across the room. Instead of a tail, it had two heads, one on either end.

"This is your room," he said. It wasn't a question. It

simply *looked* like Sera.

"When I'm here," she agreed. She went over to her bed. She paused to pet the two-headed cat. When she was done cooing at it, she knelt and dragged a chest out from under the bed.

Wen stepped over to the desk. It was covered in parchments, a handful of quills, and some bottles of ink. The parchments were full of mathematical equations, science charts, essays on the effects of sorcery, some kind of designs, and numerous other things.

"Did you do all of this?" He held up a detailed chemistry chart.

Sera barely glanced over. "Yes."

He set down the chart, picked up an essay, and started reading it. Or tried to read it—he struggled to understand all of the technical magical terms in the first paragraph. He glanced at another paper, but it was written in a completely different language—he thought it might be Elvin—and he turned away from the desk.

"May I?" He motioned to the stairs.

"Sure."

Sera stuffed a bunch of things into a bag and trailed after him up the staircase to the platform with the telescope. There was another desk up there, this one full of elaborate star charts and drawings of moons, brilliant planets, and comets. Models of these floated below the ceiling; they were suspended magically in midair and traveled in a small orbit on one side of the room.

"This was my favorite place to be when I was here." Sera ran a hand over the telescope. "Late at night, when the stars and planets were dancing in the sky. I loved watching them and charting them."

"I know two constellations," Wen admitted, "and I only know those because my father made sure I would be able to find my directions by the stars in case I was ever lost on a hunting trip when I was a child."

The faint sound of wind chimes rang through the room, and Sera moved hastily for the stairs. "That's the sound of the front gate being opened. Let's go."

11 – Love Struck

They got out of Sera's house and away from the estate without being spotted by anyone. They went to collect Bay, Sera disguised in her helmet and breastplate, and Sera took Wen to a blacksmith to get his dented shield repaired. While they were waiting on the blacksmith to finish, Sera bought a small, black mare. She made some other purchases— riding gear, saddlebags, food and other supplies—and got her horse ready to go.

"I'm going to call her Buttermelon," Sera declared as she moved her belongings from Wen's saddlebags to her own.

The mare looked at Sera as if she were out of her mind to even think of calling her such a thing. Bay huffed, and Wen said, "I think I agree with Bay. What sort of a proper horse name is Buttermelon?"

"That's rich, coming from someone who called his horse a *color* of horse."

"Actually, Bay was named after Authian Bay, which is where my castle is and where I played as a child."

"Oh." Sera began unloading the bag she'd brought from her house into the saddlebags. "Well, I think Buttermelon is a perfectly lovely name, and I'll call her Butter for short."

Butter looked slightly mollified, though Wen wasn't sure it was entirely accidental when the mare stepped on Sera's foot.

They collected Wen's repaired shield and headed for the city gates. Exiting the city proved trickier than entering it. Guards stood at the city gate now, and though they were letting people go into the city without any problems, they

93

were looking closely at anyone who went out.

"Oh, blasted bat wings! I told you my father would be looking for me." Sera touched her helmet as if to make sure it was really covering her face.

"You could turn yourself green to keep them from recognizing you," Wen suggested dryly.

"Nope. I've got a better idea. I'm glad we decided to stop by my house." Sera fished around in one of her saddlebags and pulled out a necklace with a bright sapphire in the center of it, held in place with silver twisted into a strange design.

She slid it over her head, and instantly, Wen's attention moved to the guards holding back the incoming crowd to let through some of the backed up outgoing people.

Wen moved closer to the city gates and noticed there was a mare standing very close beside Bay, but as soon as his eyes moved to the saddle, it was suddenly very important that he look somewhere else. There was a mare next to him, fine. If she wanted to leave the city, that was her business. He doubted the guards were checking horses anyway.

Wait, why were the guards looking so carefully at everyone leaving?

His mind was taunting him, telling him he knew the answer to this, that he was missing something vital and he had to find it. He glanced at the mare next to him again before his eyes *needed* to move away.

The guards examined him and let him through the gates. The mare remained at his side.

Where was he going, anyway? Why was he leaving the city?

Wen had just stopped on the road and turned his head to look back at Nayrlanda in confusion when Sera said, "I'm right here."

He whipped his head toward her as everything flooded back. She was holding the necklace in her hands.

"What is that?" he asked. "I couldn't see you. I mean, I think I could see you, but I didn't want to?"

"It's a protective necklace my brother Algernon gave me when I was little. Mother thought I might use it to cause more mayhem with my teachers, so into my chest it went." Sera tucked it back into the saddlebag. "It affects anyone in

94

the direct vicinity of the wearer. You can't really remember the person wearing it if you're near them. You probably couldn't remember why you were leaving Nayrlanda, could you?"

When Wen shook his head, she said, "That's because it was tied into your memories of me. If you'd been a little farther away from me, it wouldn't have affected you."

"I don't like that necklace." He shifted in agitation on his saddle. "I knew I was missing something important."

"It worked, though. We're free." Sera took off her helmet and attached it to a saddlebag.

"What else did you get from that chest in your room aside from money and that necklace?"

"Oh, a few trinkets. I've got some unbreakable rope, a couple of potions that might come in handy, a compass that will point you wherever you most wish to go—Mother seemed to think it would give me too many fanciful thoughts of places I could sneak off to visit. Guess she didn't think I'd just sneak off to visit them, compass or no." Sera grinned.

The rest of the morning was very pleasant, though it didn't quite wipe away his disquiet that he had, even for a few minutes, completely forgotten about Sera. He didn't know why it bothered him so much.

"Wenceslas, if you keep looking at me sideways like that, your head is going to get stuck that way," Sera said after a while.

"It is not."

"I bet I could make it get stuck that way." She tapped her club with a wicked grin.

"I'm not taking that bet," he said, but he smiled and tried to relax a little more as they traveled east.

***

They arrived in Telsa three days later. The afternoon sky was a dark, smoky gray and a light breeze played across their faces, carrying with it a promise of rain.

Telsa was a moderately sized town, and it was very easy to spot the castle. It sat in the center of town and it was surrounded by walls and walls of thick thorns, so enormous that Wen could see their sharp points from a fair distance

95

away. The town itself was very quiet; as with quite a lot of sleeping spells, the whole population had been affected. There were numerous people sleeping soundly on the streets, some in positions that looked so uncomfortable that Wen didn't blame Sera for stopping now and again to move them.

"You can just turn the thorns to feathers like you did all those plants back at that castle, right?" Wen asked.

Sera squinted doubtfully at the thorns. "I don't know." She pointed her club at the thorns as they approached. Light flooded out of it and down the plants. "Nope. My diagnostic spell tells me there's some kind of shielding spell on that thing. My magic would bounce off of it. It might turn us into feathers, and I imagine that wouldn't be very pleasant."

"Ah, well."

"A shielding spell is also going to mean it's a lot harder for you to hack through it with your sword. Those are probably going to be some tough thorns. Oh, wait, I have an idea." Sera dug into a saddlebag and emerged with a vial of clear liquid. "Here, let's stop for a minute."

They brought their horses to a halt and when Sera slid off her saddle, Wen followed suit. Sera unstoppered the bottle and handed it to Wen. "All right, you need to swallow three drops of that while facing east. As soon as you've swallowed, close your eyes and hop twice."

"With one foot or two?"

"Two feet."

"What is it I'm swallowing?"

"A strengthening potion. It will help a lot when you're trying to slice through magicked thorns." Sera took his shoulders and faced him away from the castle. "That's east."

Wen couldn't see the sun to be sure, but he trusted her sense of direction. He very carefully followed her instructions, swallowing three drops and then closing his eyes and hopping twice. A strange sensation swooped in his stomach, and when he opened his eyes, he was lightheaded.

"How do you feel?" Sera asked from behind him. "There's usually a burning feeling in your arms and legs. You should test it."

"I—" Wen stopped abruptly when he turned to face Sera.

96

A giddy, thrilling, happy bubble filled him from the inside and swelled to bursting, and a giant smile broke across his face.

"You feel that great, hm? Wenceslas? Wences—oh!" Sera's eyes went round with surprise when he lifted her off her feet and kissed her soundly on her beautiful, soft, delicate lips. Her face turned red.

"My dearest Serafina," Wen murmured. All he could think about was how amazing she was, how he could stare into those blue eyes forever, how he wanted to kiss her and kiss her until she was breathless, and he wanted—

"Wenceslas. Let me go." Sera tried to sound commanding, but her voice was more than a little dazed.

"Never." Wen's arms tightened around her. "I could never let go of a woman of such beauty and kindness and grace and *ow!*"

She had slapped him across the face, and he almost dropped her. "I'm sorry, but you needed that," she said shakily. "You're not yourself."

"Of course I'm myself! I've never been happier! I've found my love, my always and forever love, my—"

She was trembling. "If you love me, put me down at once."

Wen set Sera down instantly. She snatched the potion he hadn't realized he was still holding and smelled it. "Wenceslas, I gave you a love potion by mistake. The smells are so subtly different that I didn't notice. I don't know how my strengthening potion was switched with a—ohh, Reginald! I'll bet you anything he was getting back at me for that cockatrice...oooh, I'll throttle him when I see him next! Wh—*no,* Wenceslas!" She pushed him back as he swooped in and tried to kiss her neck.

He gave a low, desperate groan. "But I love you and I can't stand being so far away from you!"

"You're about a meter from me! And you'll stay there, do you understand me?" Sera turned to rummage through her saddlebags. "*What* I'm supposed to do—you had three drops, and with a love potion, that means three hours until it wears off; *wait* until I get my hands on Reginald! Oh, it's no use; I have nothing to counter a love potion. What am I going to do with you now?"

"Hold me. Kiss me. Tell me I'll always be yours."

"I have a better idea. Hold out your hands."

A better idea than holding or kissing or confessing undying love? Wen eagerly stuck out his hands, and Sera swiftly wrapped his wrists with rope and bound him tightly.

"Sera? Sera, what are you doing?" Wen squirmed uncomfortably. "I don't want to be tied up! How can I hold you?"

Sera pointed her club at the ground and a rosebush sprouted.

"Oh, am I going to give you flowers? Wonderful! Just untie me and I'll pick you the most splendid bouquet."

Sera smacked her club hard on the rosebush and a tree erupted from the ground, shooting up under the rosebush, completely destroying it. Wen's face fell. So much for giving Sera a bouquet.

"I'm sorry, Wenceslas. I can't have you on the loose in this state. I'd use that necklace to try to make you forget me, but it might make things worse for you. I've heard some horror stories about love potions when the object of the drinker's obsession disappears." Sera pushed him down to sit at the base of the tree. She grabbed the end of the rope around his hands, wrapped it around the tree, and tied it off. "We'll have to wait until it wears off. Make yourself comfortable."

Wen gazed at her mournfully. "You don't love me?"

"Wenceslas, I am in this town with you to get you to kiss a princess to see if you two will want to marry each other!" Sera turned her back on him and plunged her hand into her saddlebags again.

"My beloved—"

Sera swiveled back around and stuffed a handkerchief in his mouth, muffling his words. Her eyes scrunched half shut in a pained sort of way. "I'm sorry," she repeated. "You'll thank me for it when you come back to your senses."

She didn't love him. She had tied him up and gagged him and she *didn't love him.* His chest hurt so badly it was as though his heart had been ripped out and smashed and put back inside of him. He wanted to curl up and die from the agony of her rejection. Moaning, he toppled back against the tree. He couldn't even see Sera's face. She had climbed back up on Butter and had it pressed into the horse's mane.

It started to rain after a short time. Wen didn't care about the water falling down through the branches, soaking his hair and his clothes and running into his eyes. He was miserable because Sera sat, hunched and unmoving, on Butter while the rain poured over her, and he couldn't talk to her to convince her to get somewhere dry, or hold her to keep her warm in the rain. Even though she didn't love him, he wanted to prove that he could be worthy of her, that he could make her happy. What if she caught a cold sitting there getting all wet? He needed to be free so he could *help her,* but the ropes wouldn't give no matter how he tugged on them.

The rain passed, though the sky remained gray. From time to time, Sera looked over at Wen and he tried to express his devastation and longing to help in his expression, and she always turned away again.

The sky was growing darker, from night setting in, not more rain, when another odd feeling swept over him, like something rolling up all of his strong desires. It started at the top of his head, moved down his arms and chest, then his stomach and legs, until it reached his feet and dropped away.

He blinked and looked down at the ropes around his wrists, then over at Sera, practically lying across her saddle in a way that must have been very painful. Horror crept across him as all of his words and actions washed over him. They were so clear and vivid, and yet it had been as though an outsider had taken his body and used it, and now he had it back, and everything he had done and said mocked him.

Wen tried to make noise through the gag, and Sera looked over at him and straightened. "Wenceslas?" she said cautiously. "Are you back with me now?"

He nodded once, and she scrutinized him for a moment. She slid off of Butter and walked over to him. She crouched and took the handkerchief out of his mouth. She looked ready to stuff it back in if she was mistaken.

"Sera, I'm sorry."

Sera's shoulders relaxed and she shoved the handkerchief into her pocket. "It's not your fault. You didn't know it was a love potion any more than I did."

"It doesn't matter if it was a love potion. My actions hurt you whether I meant them or not. Please forgive me for that."

Sera untied the ropes around his wrists. "There's nothing to forgive. I'm sorry I hit you."

"I would have hit me, too." He tried to smile at her, but the embarrassment of what had just happened made it very difficult. "Sera, about—"

"Oh, your wrists!"

His wrists were raw and bleeding from where he'd struggled to break free of the ropes.

"Let's get inside for now, all right? The sun's already going down. We'll get dry and take care of your wrists. We can rest for tonight and start fresh in the morning. I'm sure there's an inn around here, and it's not like anyone here is going to care if we borrow some rooms for the night."

They led their wet, weary horses to find the local inn and stables. They worked in silence getting all of the gear off of the horses, brushing them down, feeding them some of the hay sitting in the corner, and making sure they had water. Once they were certain the horses were comfortable, they went over to the inn with their saddlebags in hand. There were several people sleeping in the front room at tables and on the floor behind the counter. Sera set some gold coins on the counter, and they went upstairs to find empty rooms. They found two beside each other, and once they were dried off and dressed, Sera knocked on Wen's door and came in with a jar of ointment.

"Delphina made this. It'll help your wrists." Sera motioned Wen to sit, and he did, and held his sore wrists out to her when she said, "Let's see them."

Sera pulled the lid off the jar and swiped some ointment on her fingers. She smeared it over Wen's cuts, and cool relief seeped into his wrists. The red faded away until there were no marks at all left on his arms.

"There. I told you Delphina's a fantastic healing sorceress, right?" Sera put the lid back on the jar and strode for the door. "Good night, Wenceslas."

Wen stood quickly. "Sera, wait."

Sera stopped in his doorway and turned to face him.

She was smiling, but he'd seen enough of her cheerful smiles to see how forced this one was. It didn't reach her eyes at all. "Yes?"

"About what happened. The love potion—"

"Can we just go to sleep? Please? It's been a long day and I'm tired."

He nodded. "All right. Good night, Sera."

She left, shutting his door behind herself, and he sat there staring at the closed door with something strange and wonderful and almost ferocious clawing at his chest. It reminded him a little of what he'd felt under the love potion, but much more *solid*.

He rubbed his newly healed wrists and walked over to the window in his room. The thorn-surrounded castle, cast in dark shadows, dominated the view. Somewhere in there was a princess in need of saving. A princess he would see if he liked enough to marry. As Sera had once said, someone who was fun, and colorful, and smart, and who knew his name.

Sera...

The thought of going after the princess in the castle made Wen feel more despondent than he ever had before on this giftcursed quest of his. In fact, it made him feel downright sick to his stomach.

12 – Princess of Telsa

The sun was shining brightly when morning dawned, and Sera seemed back to her normal, chipper self. She greeted Wen enthusiastically and offered him breakfast, and her eyes smiled whenever her mouth did. They ate a quick meal, fed and watered their horses, and prepared to make a run on the castle.

Sera was clad in her fighting clothes, and Wen had his sword and newly repaired shield. They left the horses in the stables and walked over to the towering layers of thorns. The thorns were different sizes, the smallest as long as his fingers and the largest as long as his arms. Their sharp points glistened dangerously. Wen and Sera couldn't find any gaps that might make less to cut through; it looked like their only choice was going to be carving entirely through to the castle.

Wen couldn't even see where the front door was, but judging from the architecture, he could make a good guess. He moved in front of that area and raised his sword. As soon as he swung the sharp blade down at the thicket of thorns, he knew this was going to be nearly impossible. The thorns barely gave at all. There was a deep scratch on some of the plants he'd hit, but his sword should have sliced cleanly through.

It took him five minutes to cut about half a meter of space, enough to take a single step.

He eyed the field of thorns. "This is going to take *forever*."

"If only Reginald hadn't taken my strengthening potion!" Sera lifted her visor. "I wonder…" She backed up and studied the thorns while Wen continued to hack away at the plants.

There were several bright flashes of light from behind him, which he recognized as Sera's use of magic. It didn't affect him, though, so he didn't look back to see what she was attempting to do until a shadow crept over his head. He looked up. A bridge of some sort was slowly coming up from the ground nearby, rising over the thorns and moving toward the high castle wall.

Sera was holding her club with both hands, and what he could see of her face through her raised visor was pinched with exertion. The bridge was made of the ground around them. It continued to grow, sucking up the earth all around it to feed itself, and spread toward the castle.

At last, the earthen bridge hit the side of the castle under a balcony. Sera's arms dropped, and she collapsed like a marionette whose strings had been cut. It reminded Wen forcefully of how weak she'd been after turning that witch in Tisi Forest into a frog.

"Sera!" Wen shoved his sword in its sheath and ran to her side. Her eyes were open and she was breathing too hard to answer him. She held up a finger.

"I'm...all right..." she finally said. "Formative spell... mixed with spell to harden bridge...exhausting..."

He propped an arm around her back and helped her sit. "That was amazing."

"Algernon...could do it...without breaking a sweat."

"You're you, not him, so don't worry about what he could or couldn't do."

"Tch. Easier said than done."

"Believe me, I know." Wen sat with his arm around Sera until her breathing had slowed. He stood when she did and waited beside her to make sure her footing was steady.

"Shall we?" She indicated the bridge.

"We shall." He walked to the bridge with her. He sincerely hoped that her magic had worked properly to make this, or they would fall a very long way down to a very bloody, painful death. He stepped onto it tentatively, and it was as hard and firm as the ground upon which he had just been walking.

Sera didn't hesitate at all; she ran swiftly up and across the bridge. He followed, growing more confident in the bridge with every step. Sera reached the balcony and swung over

103

it, and he was almost there when a horrible shriek split his ears and the bridge exploded behind him. He flung himself toward the balcony and his hand closed on the railing right before the bridge collapsed underneath him. He gripped it tightly with his fingers, swinging his other arm up to hold on to the edge with both hands. Sera grabbed his arms and shouted something, but it was drowned out by that horrible screaming.

Wen looked wildly around and immediately spotted the source of the noise. A monstrous creature had risen out of a clear space between the castle and the thorns. It had a body that reminded him a little bit of a dragon, but sleeker and without all of the ridges and spikes. It made up for the lack of spikes with its heads—it had too many for Wen to count, because they kept moving around each other like some kind of gruesome, undulating snakes. Each head had a mouth full of teeth that were longer than any of the thorns below.

Wen scrabbled to pull himself over the balcony. Sera frantically yanked him, and he got himself over as two of the heads snapped at him. He shoved Sera back as one head chomped down on the balcony and devoured half of it in a single gulp, just missing Wen's feet.

The second head came for them. Wen and Sera fell backward and crashed through the balcony door into a room in the castle. It didn't stop the monster, which broke through the castle wall as easily as if it were made out of sand.

Wen and Sera dragged each other up and ran for a door, but a monster neck whirled in front of them and the face turned to them, screeching.

"Where did that thing come from!?" Wen shouted.

"I don't know! This was *not* in the report!" They barely missed being eaten by a head that came down toward the top of them. Wen yanked out his sword and slashed blindly, and he was pretty sure he hit it in the eye. Blue blood splashed across Sera's arm.

She screamed and dropped her club. "Ahhh, it's burning me!"

There were three heads surrounding them in the room now, all of them rearing back like snakes getting ready to strike. Sera uttered little cries of pain as she wiped off the blood on her arm. She dove for her club as one head came at her. It slammed against her and she smacked into the wall. The other two went for Wen, who launched himself into a somersault. The two monster skulls collided and screeched so loudly his ears rang.

Sera clambered off the floor, and Wen kicked her club to her. She snatched it up and jabbed it outward. A jet of boiling water hissed through the air and struck two of the heads. They writhed and wheeled backward. Wen grabbed Sera's arm and pulled her toward the door. Another head smashed through the wall, cutting them off from running down a corridor, and they threw themselves into a door opposite the one they'd just left.

And there was their sleeping princess, lying serenely on a bed surrounded by gauzy, white material. Wen got a brief glimpse of her long, black hair spread perfectly on her pillow and her hands folded on top of her chest before more of the monsters broke into the room, spraying it with debris from the wall.

"Wenceslas! Wake her up; we need to get her out of here!" Sera flipped over a monster neck and swung her club at a head that came toward her. She almost lost an arm. A bunch of sparkly stars spewed out of the end of her club, and she shouted in frustration.

Wen darted forward and hacked at the monster attacking Sera. A deep gouge appeared in its neck, and more blue blood sprayed out across the ground.

"WENCESLAS! HURRY UP AND KISS THE BLASTED PRINCESS ALREADY!" Sera screamed. "I'VE GOT THIS!" A giant spider shot out of her club and landed on the monster, which promptly ate the spider.

Wen hesitated only a moment then jumped onto the bed, tearing down the pretty white bed hangings. He ripped them off the princess, took one look at her peaceful, porcelain face, and kissed her ruby red lips.

Her eyes blinked open and widened when Wen grabbed her and rolled off the bed. Monster teeth clamped on the bed and snapped it in half, showering Wen and the princess with splinters of wood, feathers from the mattress, and shreds of material.

Wen got a glimpse of the head Sera had been fighting, and a surge of terror hit him as he saw her leg jutting out between two teeth in its mouth; her club lay on the ground. He dropped the princess and leapt toward that head, his voice raw as it tore from his throat. *"Sera!"*

He leapt over one neck, slashed at another monster face, and jumped onto the long, undulating neck of the monster that had eaten Sera. He slammed his sword into its neck, over and over, splattering himself with blood that burned and blistered on his skin, until the severed head dropped to the ground. He leapt off the neck as it writhed in death throes.

For a moment, he was surrounded by sharp teeth and screeching, and then suddenly all of the heads froze. They straightened up, backed away from Wen, and swayed gently to some kind of woodwind music flooding through the room.

The princess was standing beside the bed, playing into an ocarina, her eyes fixed on the monsters. She glanced quickly at Wen and nodded at him reassuringly.

Wen lunged at the severed monster head; Sera's leg was still jammed between two teeth. He thought he might throw up. Had it eaten most of her and left her leg behind? "Sera!" *No, no, no, no...*

He froze, glorious relief sweeping over him, when Sera's muffled voice said, "Wenceslas? Mind helping me out of this thing? My leg is stuck."

The princess was still playing the ocarina, walking around the bed toward Wen with an expression of concern on her face, but he barely noticed. He worked on prying open the mouth of the head he'd chopped off. With teeth as long as he was, pushing open the mouth was no simple feat. He had to roll the head onto its side, slowly so Sera had time to shift with the movement, and then get it propped open.

Sera peered out at him from the side of the monster's mouth. Its massive, forked tongue lay across her stomach and her leg stuck up awkwardly because of how it was pinned between the teeth, but she was wonderfully, beautifully *alive*.

Wen managed to get Sera unstuck only by breaking one of the teeth holding her. He kicked it until it moved enough

106

for her leg to slip out. Sera wiggled her way past the other saber-like teeth and out of the mouth. She was scratched and bloodied and one of her arms was severely burned, but the wide-eyed way she was looking at him made him wonder what sort of state he was in. He still had thick, gooey monster blood splashed on him, and he wiped at it with his shirt. Underneath it, he was badly burned. His heart was racing and his blood pumping, and he was pretty sure that was numbing the pain he should have been feeling.

The princess was the only one in the room who was untouched; she looked almost surreal in her silvery gown. A simple tiara was pinned to her dark hair, and she motioned with one hand for Sera and Wen to follow her. Sera scooped her club off the ground. She took one step, cried out, and fell to the floor.

"My leg..." she said as Wen crouched beside her. Only then did he see the blood soaking the inside of her trousers. The cloth had been sliced through and she had a long, mangled gash on the inside of her leg.

Wen picked her up and cradled her carefully to him. Her breastplate dug into his ribs and her helmet pressed into his shoulder. The princess waited for him and then led the way out of the room and down the corridor. They had to climb over a long, swaying monster neck, and then they moved quickly down a spiral staircase. After a short time, from somewhere far above, the screeches of the monster and the sound of breaking rock returned as it resumed its smashing of the castle.

"It must be out of hearing range now." The princess lowered her ocarina. She sighed and leaned against the wall. "I'm so sorry you had to face that horrible creature."

"If I'd known it liked music, I'd have conjured an instrument," Sera said weakly. "That was so much worse than a dragon or a troll or a crazy centaur. Worse than my father, even. What *was* it?"

The princess continued down the staircase and exited into another corridor with Wen on her heels. His fight-or-flight response was starting to wear off and all of the aches and burns he'd suffered were making themselves very, very known.

"You should know that this castle is surrounded by

thorns," Wen said. "There's no way out."

"What?" The princess's shoulders sagged, but only for a moment. "Oh, he's a tricky one. Fortunately, I don't think he knew about the secret passage to the miller's. Come on." She turned a different direction. They passed several frightened servants who had obviously just awakened, and the princess urged them to follow her.

The servants hastily fell in behind her, wincing as more faint monster screams echoed around them and the sounds of destruction continued from above.

"To answer your question, that monstrosity is Quentin's pet," the princess said sourly as she continued onward with Wen, Sera, and the servants.

"Quentin?" Sera stirred in Wen's arms. "I knew a Quentin once. Prince Quentin of Hollin's End."

"That's him," the princess said grimly. "He is out of control."

"Who is he?" Wen asked.

"Do you remember when I told you I'd met a seventh son of a seventh son who had a penchant for turning people into glass when he breathed on them?" Sera asked. "That was Quentin of Hollin's End."

"Except he doesn't have to breathe on people to turn them into glass; that was just what amused him the most. I don't know when it was that you met him, but he's been getting worse and worse over the past months," the princess explained. "He overthrew his father and banished all his brothers to gain control of the kingdom."

She grabbed a torch from the wall and snapped her fingers, and a flame sprang to life on the end of it. She pulled open a heavy door and led the way into a dank tunnel.

"He doesn't really turn people into glass anymore unless they upset him or he's in a funny mood," the princess said. "I think he realized he had to have people in his kingdom if he wanted to rule them. He turned pretty much everything else to glass, though—the houses, the fountains, the roads, the trees and plants."

"How impractical," Sera muttered.

"I completely agree." A rat scurried past and the princess stepped neatly around it. "He took a fancy to me on one of my kingdom's diplomatic trips to his castle. He wanted my hand in marriage, and my father said he would have to consider, though he would have sooner turned himself into a pig than let me marry Quentin. I have some magic of my own, and I heard the winds speak of Quentin's sorceress coming to put a sleeping spell on the castle."

"You're a wind hearer?" Sera said in surprise. "That's a really rare gift among those with sorcery."

"I'm only a bit of one," the princess said modestly. "Enough to hear things from time to time. I didn't hear anything about the monster, but Quentin must have set it to guard this place from anyone. He wanted to come and *rescue* me himself, you see, and make it out that he was the noble one in all of this. He didn't know I was aware he was the one behind it. My father took some of his knights and soldiers and went to seek help from some of the neighboring kingdoms. He hoped if they joined together, they might be able to put a stop to Quentin. The day the sleeping enchantment fell upon us, one of my father's messengers returned to tell me that Quentin had found out about it and turned Father into glass."

"I'm sorry," Sera said quietly. "There should be a way to restore him, if you can find him."

"Yes, I know." The princess squared her shoulders. "And I will, if it's the last thing I do."

The tunnel sloped upward and ended in a trapdoor above them. Wen lifted Sera into the mill and climbed up after her, and the princess assisted the group of servants in getting out. Wen's body was screaming at him now from all the places the monster's blood had burned.

"We should be far enough from the castle to avoid that creature," the princess said. "I need to check on my subjects in town now that they'll all be waking up, and I'll need to gather together my soldiers to take care of the monster. I'm sure there are still people trapped in the castle."

"If you play your music, it might be easy for a group of people to slay it," Sera suggested.

"Exactly what I was thinking. In the meantime, you two should tend to your wounds," the princess said.

"We need to get back to the inn. My ointment is there," Sera said.

"I'll come see you there later, once I've taken care of this mess," the princess replied. "I very much wish to speak with you more. And please, excuse my manners, I didn't even introduce myself. I'm Princess Jessalin, sole heir to the throne of Telsa."

"I'm Wenceslas, seventh prince of Eirdane." Wen picked up Sera again, his arms protesting every movement. "This is—" He glanced down at Sera, unsure how she wished to be introduced.

"Sera," she supplied. "From Nayrlanda."

"Wenceslas, Sera, thank you again," Jessalin said. "Now, please, go see to your injuries."

Wen and Sera returned to the inn through a town that was coming out of its slumber. Children chattered, men and women called to each other, a baby's wail pierced the air, a dog barked.

The innkeeper, dazed and sleepy-eyed, was examining the gold coins that Sera had left on the counter when Wen carried her inside. After quickly explaining that they had left the gold in exchange for rooms and that they had broken the spell on the town, the innkeeper was more than happy to allow them to return to their rooms. Though she might have just been anxious to keep them from dripping blood all over the place.

Wen went straight into Sera's room and set her on the bed. She put down her club and took off her helmet and placed it beside her. Her smattering of freckles stood out starkly on her far-too-pale face. The breastplate came off next. Grimacing, Sera pulled out her jar of ointment. "Shirt off, please," she said tiredly. "It's covered in monster blood."

Wen carefully removed his shirt, trying his best not to transfer any of the blood he'd wiped on it to his skin.

Sera's eyes flickered to his chest, then quickly away. She patted the bed. "Sit." Wen sat, and Sera opened the jar and put it between them. Sera handled the gash on her leg first, sighing in relief as she smoothed the ointment on the deep cut. She and Wen spent the next few minutes rubbing the ointment on themselves and each other, as they could see the full extent of one another's injuries better than they could see them on themselves.

"So," Sera said, dabbing ointment on Wen's shoulder, "what did you think of Princess Jessalin?"

"She's nice." Wen gently brushed ointment across a cut on Sera's cheek. It instantly faded away. "She's a lot different from most princesses I've met."

"Different from most I've met, too. Look up." Coolness spread through a burn on Wen's neck as Sera's fingers made circles on it. "She's a decent sorceress, too—she lit the fire on that torch without needing any wand or other magic enhancer."

Silence fell as they finished medicating the rest of their wounds. Wen scraped the excess ointment from his fingers back into the jar and Sera sealed it.

"I thought it had eaten you," he said quietly. "The monster."

"It sure tried." Sera bounced up from the bed and walked to the window. "I almost got us killed in there because my stupid magic wouldn't do what I wanted it to."

"You saved me when you hit those two heads with hot water."

"I didn't do that on purpose." She folded her arms on the windowsill, her back to Wen. "At least we got out of there alive, *and* you broke the enchantment!" She turned back around, smiling—but it was the same fake sort of smile she'd worn yesterday after the love potion debacle. "So there's that." She glanced down at herself. "I need to change. Make myself presentable. Jessalin is supposed to visit us later." She shooed Wen toward the door. "You should do the same; you're a wreck."

She nudged him out into the hallway and shut him out, leaving him standing outside her door with a heaviness and longing on his heart.

13 – Faerie Field

Princess Jessalin came to see them in the inn that afternoon, as promised. "I would normally invite you to an audience in the castle," she said as she sat on a chair Sera offered her. Sera perched on her bed and Wen remained standing. "But we still haven't found a way to remove the thorns. At least my soldiers were able to dispense with that horrible creature. Castle repairs will take quite a while once we can find a way to rid ourselves of the thorns. The monster did a lot of damage, but fortunately, it seems everyone's lives were spared."

"What are you going to do next?" Wen asked.

"I sent a messenger to Nayrlanda University with word about Quentin and asked for any aid they can provide. I just..." Jessalin's voice broke and tears shined in her brown eyes. "I fear for my father."

Sera dug into the pocket of her blue dress, the only clothes she had left now that her trousers had been ruined, and pulled out a handkerchief. She handed it to Jessalin, who thanked her and dabbed at her eyes with it. "I haven't had a chance to ask you both why you risked your lives so valiantly to awaken me." She folded the handkerchief neatly and set it beside her on the chair.

Wen and Sera looked at each other. Sera made a 'go ahead' motion with her hands, and Wen shifted from one foot to the other, undecided.

"Oh, for the love of dragons, Wenceslas," she grumbled. "He's under a fairy godmother enchantment," Sera blurted, waving at Wen. "It makes it so he has to leave his castle and go on a quest to attempt to fulfill it."

"A fairy godmother enchantment of what sort? One that requires breaking spells on kingdoms?" Jessalin asked curiously.

"On princesses," Wen said with a sigh.

Jessalin looked alarmed. "For how long are you to do this?"

"Until he can get a princess to marry him or he turns seventeen and pricks his finger on a glass coffin and falls into an enchanted sleep," Sera said.

"Oh. Oh!" Jessalin blinked at Wen, and then her cheeks reddened a little. "I see," she said softly. "And how long until you're seventeen?"

"Nine days," Wen said.

"That's not much time." Jessalin considered him. "You said you're the seventh prince of Eirdane? That's the kingdom by the sea, isn't it? At Authian Bay?"

"Yes. You know it?" Wen asked in surprise. There were so many kingdoms that most people who weren't in the vicinity of Eirdane paid it little notice. It was a pretty quiet kingdom, on the whole.

Jessalin smiled. "My mother was courted by one of the princes of Eirdane, long ago. Frederick, I believe."

"My uncle," Wen said.

Sera looked between the two of them. Jessalin's gaze shifted over to her. "It doesn't explain your part in the journey."

"My part's really not much," Sera said. "We met fighting a dragon and we've been helping each other out since."

"It is *not* 'not much,'" Wen protested. "Sera has saved me on more than one occasion, and I never would have rescued you without her."

Jessalin nodded once. "I see." She sat still, regarding Wen as if trying to see into the very depths of his soul. "Prince Wenceslas—"

"Wen."

"Wen," she said. "I have a favor to ask. I know you have already done me unimaginable service. If you would do me one greater, I will agree to marry you in time to spare you from your enchantment. I'm sure my father wouldn't protest."

Sera went still and Wen's heart thumped loudly in his

ears. This was what he had been trying to do for years, wasn't it? And this princess was smart, nice, and articulate, and she put her people first.

He considered her, and without agreeing, questioned, "What is it you would ask of me?"

"I wish to know where my father is and if he can be restored. I recall seeing a room of glass statues when I visited the castle at Hollin's End. It could be that Quentin keeps the people he turns to glass there for some kind of sick amusement."

"He did always find that very funny," Sera said. "The university in Nayrlanda had to intervene a couple of years ago and restore all the people he had changed."

"I would go after my father myself, but my people are looking to me to reestablish order and they're frightened knowing my father has gone missing." Jessalin picked up the handkerchief and pressed it again to her eyes.

Sera looked at Wen, her expression unreadable, and he stared back at her, his forehead furrowed. "I..." He trailed off, and then tried again. "I don't..."

Sera sighed, jumped off the bed, and said, "Will you excuse us for a moment?"

"Of course," Jessalin said.

Sera seized Wen's arm and pulled him out of her room. She shut the door and whispered, "What is it about this one, then?"

"What?"

"Don't you *what* me. You know exactly what. What is it about this princess that's making you hesitate?"

The crease in Wen's forehead deepened.

"If you don't think she's right for you, all right, but... look at her, Wenceslas! You said it yourself: She's different from other princesses you've met. She's smart, she can say your name, she's kind and caring, and even though she's exhausted and worried, she's holding herself together beautifully. Most princesses would be a blubbering mess right now. When she woke up to a monster attacking, she kept her head and tamed it instead of panicking and screaming."

Wen's eyes drifted to the door. "I know."

"Just answer me this. Do you think you would be miserable marrying her?"

Wen's eyes snapped back to Sera. His voice lodged somewhere in his throat. It took him two tries to get it to work again. "I don't know if miserable is the right word—"

"Well, then, what are you standing around out here for? Hollin's End is three or four days from here with some good riding." Sera's arms folded tightly across her chest. "If we leave *right now*, we'll only have one or two days to try to find out what happened to her father and leave to get back here by your seventeenth birthday. And that's if nothing goes wrong. You're on a very, very tight schedule here."

Wen could take a hint or three. "Sera, I made you a promise that I would help you find something to run toward." He shook his head. "I'm not turning my back on that."

Her face tightened, only for a moment, and then a smile flashed across her face. "Of course you're not," she said lightly. "I'll come with you to Hollin's End. I have my end of this to uphold, too. You're not safely awake past your seventeenth birthday yet." She opened the door to her room and stepped back inside.

Wen followed and walked over to Princess Jessalin. He took her hand and kissed it. "I'm willing to see if I can find your father in exchange for your hand in marriage." His stomach plunged somewhere to the vicinity of his toes. He slid a sideways glance at Sera, but she was digging through her things, her back to him.

"I accept," Jessalin said with great dignity. Then her face crumpled in relief. "Thank you. Please let me know if you need any supplies before you go."

***

Bay and Butter kept up a steady pace as they traveled away from Telsa. Wen glanced back from time to time and watched the thorn-surrounded castle get smaller and smaller, until it wasn't even a dot in the distance anymore. The farther they traveled, the lighter Wen felt. Here on the open road, he could almost pretend he was still on a seemingly hopeless quest to rescue and marry a princess. He could almost pretend he hadn't just agreed to an offer of marriage.

115

Sera was uncharacteristically subdued when they started out, but even she perked up after a while. By the time they'd had lunch, she was humming under her breath.

"On the bright side, you don't have to go see those twelve dancing princesses," Sera said as they plodded onward through some woods under the sunny sky. "On the not-so-bright side, we're going to pay a visit to a prince who likes turning people into glass."

"Who's also a seventh son of a seventh son. One with actual powers," Wen pointed out. "Unlike me."

Sera sat on her saddle in her breastplate and brand-new trousers, courtesy of Jessalin, who had not questioned at all why Sera wanted them. She was holding a compass and gazing down at it with a slight frown on her face.

"Wenceslas, if Quentin has turned so much to glass, there very well may be glass coffins lying around. If we don't get out of there before your birthday, this is probably the worst place you could be. Not that your enchantment wouldn't be fulfilled even if you were in the middle of a forest; I just don't want to lug your sleeping body all the way back to Telsa to get Princess Jessalin to kiss you awake."

Wen tried to imagine Jessalin kissing him awake from an enchanted sleep. True love's kiss. Except he didn't think Jessalin's kiss was going to do much should he fall asleep.

"Wenceslas? Did you hear me?"

"Yes. We'll just try to be in and out quickly." He didn't want to talk about it anymore. He hastily changed the subject. "Is that the compass that points toward the place you most want to go?" He was sure it must be. Sera didn't need a regular compass.

"Yes." Sera tucked it quickly into her pocket.

"Where *do* you most want to go?" he asked curiously.

"Oh, lots of places," she said airily. "There are so many things I haven't seen that I would love to explore. The crystal caverns at Montegue, the faerie field on the floating city of Berush, the musical symposium of wood elves in Helane... oh, Wenceslas, there are so many places I've always wanted to see. What about you? If you could go one place right now, where would it be?"

Anywhere, as long as it's with you. Wen's unguarded thought was as blinding and obvious as the sun shining

116

overhead. It made him simultaneously giddy and horribly depressed, because Sera...Sera was only there to help him break his giftcurse, and because she was looking for what she really wanted. She was trying to help him marry Jessalin. She had *encouraged* him to pursue Jessalin, had listed off all the princess's positive traits.

Wen's shoulders slumped.

"Wenceslas?"

Sera was still waiting for an answer. He looked down at his hands holding the reins. Sera was here with him for now, and he would have to accept that and figure out how to say goodbye when the time came.

"I suppose if I had to pick one place, it would be home." He smiled wistfully. "I've spent so many years not being able to stay there that it's often the place I most want to be."

"And I've spent so many years being trapped by my home that it's the last place I want to be."

"I think you might like mine," he said. "The beach and the fields—there's not a wood elf symposium, but there are musicals and street fairs. I used to dress up in raggedy clothes and smear dirt on my face so I could sneak into the fairs without being noticed as a prince."

Sera laughed. "Nice to know I'm not the only one who goes incognito to avoid attention."

"You should come visit with me. Mum would adore you. Did I tell you she was a giant slayer before she met Dad?"

"She *was?*"

"She always says it was good preparation for having seven boys."

Sera grinned, and then her smile slipped and she looked determinedly ahead. "As lovely as that sounds, Wenceslas— watch out!"

She yanked on her reins. Butter reared, barely keeping from trampling the man who suddenly threw himself out of the woods and onto the road in front of them.

Wen brought Bay to a quick halt and slid off, his hand going to the hilt of his sword. The man lying on the road wore torn, tattered clothes and looked as though he'd taken a dip in a mud bath, rolled down a grassy hill, and then jumped in a briar patch. His shoulder-length hair was tangled and matted, and Wen wasn't sure if it was naturally brown or just that dirty.

"Hello?" Wen said cautiously.

The man groaned into the dirt.

Wen didn't see any weapons in his hands, splayed out across the ground. He crouched down beside the man, and Sera dropped down on his other side.

"Are you all right?" Sera asked. "Where did you come from?"

The man mumbled something, and Wen and Sera looked at each other.

"Did he say he escaped the mental institution in Rie's Beach or the minstrel institution in Briar Leaf?" Wen asked.

"I don't know." Sera lightly touched the man's shoulder. "My vote's on the minstrel institution. I knew this harpist once; the things he said they put him through..." She shook her head. "Here, help me roll him over."

They rolled the man onto his back and he stared up at them, glassy-eyed. "So...many...ballads..."

"Definitely the minstrel institution," Sera muttered. "It's all right, darling," she said gently to the man. "You're going to be just fine."

"Songs...can't stop hearing them...in my sleep...when I'm awake...limericks..." The man groaned and his eyes rolled back in his head.

"Hmm." Sera sat back on her heels. She and Wen jumped when the man sat bolt upright with a piercing scream and then fell back on the ground with his eyes closed.

"He needs help," Sera said in a hushed tone. "I don't know what happened to him, but—"

The man's eyes snapped open. He burst into limerick.

"There were twelve princesses
Danced away with witlessness
Who every night
Could not fight
And so wore out their shoeses"

Wen raised his eyebrows. "Shoeses?"

"We heard about those princesses," Sera said to the man. "In Quells, right? We even met one of them, we think. Esme." She pulled out her club and pointed it at the man while she was talking.

"Yes, Esme!" the man said. "Third...sister..."

Light flooded over him from Sera's club, and she frowned. "You've got some kind of spell on you, but it's all muddled. Kind of like...a spell holding you back, holding you to something?"

"Yes." The man gasped and grabbed Sera's arm. "Institution...the king..."

"What king?" Wen asked.

Another limerick spilled from the man.

"The king of Quells was disillusioned
With the man his daughter affectioned
The king did imprison him
To a life of eternal hymn
In the old minstrel institution"

"Ahh," Sera said. "So the king of Quells arranged for you to be bound to the minstrel institution?"

The man groaned. "My poor Delia. I cannot save her... dancing..." He collapsed onto his back once more. "So tired. So hard to fight the pull."

"The pull to go back to the institution. Do you know if there was a fulfillment to this spell? A way to break it?"

"Death," the man gasped.

"How very cheerful," Wen muttered. With a king like that, he was rather glad he wasn't going to have to go to Quells in search of marriage to one of the twelve princesses.

Sera tapped her club on the ground, considering. There was a flash of light, and a flurry of spiders appeared from her club. She quickly stopped tapping. Nodding, she stood and went to her saddlebags. She came back with a tiny bottle of potion.

"I have enough of this potion for one use," she told the man. "It's really, really rare. It will remove one spell, as long as it's not caused by fairy godmother magic." She gave Wen a quick look as though to assure him that's why she hadn't offered it to him. "I got it on my fourth birthday and I've been saving it for something really important. And...well, I don't know what's more important than love." She unstoppered the bottle and held it to the man's mouth. "Drink all

119

of it."

The potion emptied into his mouth and he swallowed reflexively. His whole body went rigid, and then he relaxed and the dazed look in his eyes cleared. He sat up slowly. "I'm...I'm free?" He burst into loud, dry sobs and flung his arms around Sera. "Thank you. Thank you, thank you, you wonderful girl!"

Sera patted him on the back. "Don't let it go to waste, please."

"I won't, I promise you." The man pulled back and wiped his dirty face with equally dirty hands, which really did nothing at all for him. "I fell in love with my beloved Delia long ago, and I have been locked in the minstrel institution for countless months. When word reached us of the twelve dancing princesses, I knew I had to escape. I had to save my beloved. Don't worry, I am prepared! I met a kind woman on the road right after I left the institution, and she gave me a cloak of invisibility. I will rescue Delia if it's the last thing I do!"

Jumping up, he swooped down and kissed Sera on the cheek, shook Wen's hand enthusiastically, and set off down the road on foot.

"That was really generous of you to give him that potion," Wen said as they mounted their horses again. He and Sera waved at the man as they overtook and passed him.

"He needed it," she said simply. "Who knows if I ever really would have? I just hope things work out for him. To be separated from the one you love until you die because of some spell—it's horrible. Sometimes magic can be used for really awful things, Wenceslas."

"Like turning everything into glass?"

"Oh, speaking of which, I've been thinking about how we should approach Quentin. I think we should go to see him in high style as—well, as ourselves. Instead of sneaking, a diplomatic trip might be our best excuse to poke around. A lot of princes are arrogant pigs—no offense—and this one certainly is. We'll play on his—"

"—hubris?" Wen inserted dryly.

"Yes," she said with a small laugh.

"Sounds good, but I don't have anything appropriate to

wear for a high-style diplomatic trip to a neighboring kingdom."

"Me, neither. We should stop somewhere along the way and buy some really fancy clothing."

"Sounds like a good plan."

They rode on for several more hours until the sun started to go down, and then they set up camp in the pink and green grass of a faerie field. Several curious faeries flew around them, but ultimately decided they weren't very interesting and left them alone.

Bursts of light from the faeries began to flash around the field as the sky grew darker. Wen and Sera unloaded their horses, brushed them down, and checked their hooves for stones. When the sun had completely set and the stars were twinkling overhead, the faeries in one corner started a dance. The swirl of brilliant lights coming from that area was entrancing.

"Looks like they're having a great party over there," Wen said.

"Hm?" Sera looked up from her magic compass.

"I said it looks like they're having a great party over there." Wen nodded toward the faeries. "That compass must be really fascinating, the way you keep pulling it out to stare at it."

"Oh. It's...yes." Sera folded her fingers around the compass.

"Are you hoping it might tell you what you most want to run toward? I don't think that's something any magical object can tell you."

Sera didn't respond to that. She tucked the compass away and rolled onto her stomach on her blanket. "Good night, Wenceslas."

"Good night, Sera."

She soon fell asleep with her knees tucked under her. Wen stayed awake for a long time, watching Bay and Butter munching on the grass, and the faeries dancing, and Sera sleeping.

He whipped his head in the direction of a sudden, soft giggling near his ear. Two faeries floated before him, one with shocking pink hair and the other with pale blue hair, both with a faint glow around them.

121

"Ooh, you're right!" the pink-haired faerie said. "He's handsome for a human."

The blue-haired one wiggled her fingers at Wen and giggled again. "Hi, handsome human. You're looking awfully melancholy over here. You should be celebrating! It's a beautiful night, and the stars are dancing with us, and—"

"—and she may have had a bit too much nectar, if you know what I mean," the pink-haired faerie whispered conspiratorially, tipping back her fingers toward her mouth.

The blue-haired faerie elbowed her friend.

"Ahem," the pink-haired faerie said. "What I mean is, why are you looking so glum?"

Wen's eyes moved to Sera, and the two faeries followed his line of sight. "Oooh!" squealed the blue-haired faerie. "Let me guess! She's your betrothed and you two are on a harrowing journey to save her from a horrendous curse placed on her by a demented witch!"

"Not exactly," Wen said with some amusement. "I'm under a fairy godmother enchantment—"

Both faeries winced. "Oh, dear, is it dreadful?" the pink-haired one asked.

"Of course it must be dreadful, Niamin, look at his face!" the blue-haired faerie said. "See how sad he is! Fairy godmothers, psht! They're not even proper faeries, are they, they just steal our name and don't even spell it right and—"

"Shh, Melila, I want to know about it!" Niamin waved at her friend.

"It's kind of complicated," Wen said, because both faeries were staring at him with wide, expectant eyes, though Melila's eyes kept crossing, no doubt due to her consumption of too much nectar. "I'm supposed to break a spell on a princess and marry her by the time I turn seventeen, and I did part of that and may very well do the other half on time, but..." His gaze flickered to Sera again. "But I would trade all my kingdom for a..." *Sorceress,* he finished silently, unable to voice it. *One very special, amazing, unmatched sorceress. I would give anything just to—* "Newt!"

"For a newt?" Niamin asked, and then screamed when Wen grabbed her and Melila just as a red-orange newt snapped at the air right where the two faeries had been. It was the biggest Wen had ever seen, standing as tall as his knees.

"Newt!" the faeries shrieked, and as soon as Wen released them, they flew high into the sky. The newt opened his mouth and a burst of flame shot out of it.

"Fire newt!" the faeries screamed, and they pelted the newt with colorful sparks. The newt snapped at them, then turned and bolted away through the grass. The faeries chased after it, showering it with sparks until it was out of their field.

Sera stirred and mumbled something in her sleep.

The faeries flew back over to Wen and brushed their wings against his cheeks, a sort of faerie kiss. "Thank you!" Melila cried. "You saved our lives."

Niamin glanced over her shoulder at the faerie party still happening in the far corner of the field. "Look, we aren't normally supposed to do things like this, but I think you've earned it. In return for saving our lives. Hold out your hand."

Wen held out his hand, palm up, and the pink-haired faerie pressed both her hands against his. His hand began to glow, and for a moment, he was terrified she was going to give him some magical "gift" that he could sooner do without. It was too late to do anything about it, and anyway, turning down faerie gifts was generally a very unwise thing. He calmed when he reminded himself that they *really* weren't fairy godmothers.

"There." Niamin flew back and graced him with a smile. "That's good for one time only, so use it well. If ever you or someone near you is in great need, press your hand to your heart or to the heart of the person you want to protect and say my name, Niamin. You, or the person you touch, will be protected from all harm for one hour, be it magic or sword or anything else."

Wen stared at his hand. "Thank you."

"Thank *you*. And cheer up, all right? Nothing is so bad that you can't sort it out."

Melila giggled. "Or have some nectar and then nothing really looks bad."

Waving at him, the faeries flew lazily across the field back toward their party.

14 – Hollin's End

It was easy to spot Hollin's End from very far away. Everything within and around the city glittered and gleamed under the afternoon sunlight. The road Wen and Sera were on soon turned into glass that threw off reflections. There were cracks and numerous places where the glass had been chipped away by travelers. Bay and Butter didn't seem terribly thrilled with it, but they plodded onward determinedly as they traveled toward the city itself. The trees along the road were unmoving in their frozen glass states, and not a blade of green grass could be seen anywhere.

They soon entered the city. Glass cottages, wells, and clotheslines were everywhere they looked. There weren't many people out on the streets, and those they did pass were jumpy and alarmed and quickly ducked their heads when Wen and Sera passed.

"Turn back!" One old, gnarled man hobbled up to them, using a cane to walk. "This isn't anywhere you want to visit! It may look like a beauty from a distance, but the heart of this city is black and ugly."

"We know," Sera said. "Prince Quentin—"

Everyone within hearing distance gasped and the old man replied, "*King* Quentin, miss! He hears you call him prince, he'll turn you to glass faster than you can say pumpkin!"

"He's a usurper who stole his father's crown and banished all his brothers. I'll call him whatever I wish," Sera said.

The townsfolk all ducked their heads and turned away, and the old man shook his head sadly and backed away from Wen and Sera. "On your own head be it."

The rest of the city was much the same. Wen and Sera grew closer and closer to the castle, towering above the rest of the city, a monumental glass building with towers, spires, and turrets.

"You ready for this?" Sera asked.

She was almost unrecognizable as the trouser-wearing, helmeted girl he'd met fighting a dragon a couple of weeks before. They had stopped two days earlier to purchase new clothing, and Sera had bought a fitted blue gown, covered in jewels and with rows of pearls swirling across it. For the first time since Wen had met her, she truly looked like part of high society. Her hair was tied up in a fancy little twist, and the only thing that remained of her unconventional appearance were the wispy bangs that dangled above her eyes and the club strapped to her hip. She had moved all of her important trinkets to a bag that was tied around her waist and hung from her other hip.

Wen tugged on the white gloves covering his fingers. "Yes."

"Also, remember that if Quentin breathes on you, it won't turn you into glass unless he wants it to happen. He can also snap his fingers or wave his hand and hit you with a glass spell. Let's hope we don't make him upset and that he's not in a funny mood."

"Are you really going to irritate him by calling him a prince?"

"Only if he makes me really mad and I have good reason to."

They stopped at the castle gate, which was closed and guarded by several wary-looking soldiers. "Halt!" One soldier held up his hand and a sword. "Who goes there?"

"I am Serafina Nayrlanda, sorceress of the same city, and this is my companion, Prince Wenceslas of Eirdane. We request to see the ruler of this grand city."

The soldiers murmured among themselves and at last opened the gate. "Leave your horses here, please. I'll escort you in."

Wen and Sera dismounted and followed the soldier who had spoken.

"You have no idea," Sera muttered to Wen, "how difficult

it was to refrain from introducing you as Winning Loss."

"I appreciate your restraint," he said dryly.

"I can't help it! You have the best name ever." She skipped once, then seemed to remember she was supposed to be looking dignified and tilted her chin up and slowed her step.

The castle's walls were so thick that Wen couldn't see through the glass. His footsteps echoed in the halls as the soldier led them through the castle, past tapestries, decorations, and suits of armor that had all been turned into glass. Instead of being beautiful, the effect was to make everything look wrong and rather eerie.

The soldier stopped in front of huge double doors and said something quietly to two other soldiers who stood there. They opened the doors. "Please wait here," said their escort. Wen got a brief glimpse of an audience chamber with a glass throne at the end of it, and a man sitting on the throne, before their escort stepped inside and the door was closed again.

It wasn't long until the soldier reemerged. "King Quentin will see you now."

The door was pulled open wide, and Wen stepped through with Sera. He studied Quentin as he approached the throne. The self-declared king was about Wen's age, maybe a little older, with dark hair, a very angular chin, and brooding eyes.

"Your majesty," Sera said, "how good to see you again."

"Ahh, Serafina Nayrlanda." Quentin rose from his throne and came down to greet her. He took her hand and Wen stiffened, but Quentin kissed her hand instead of turning her into glass. "How marvelous to see you again."

"I'm surprised you remember me."

"One never forgets a visit from any member of the Nayrlanda family, particularly when that person turned his brother into a dog."

Sera cleared her throat. "That was an accident."

"A very fortunate one. He needed to be put in his place." A thin smile curled Quentin's mouth and he turned to Wen. "And you are a prince of—I'm sorry, where was it?"

"Eirdane."

Quentin's response was lazy and dismissive. "Never

heard of it." He looked between them. "What brings you to my glorious kingdom?" He gave Sera a rather sly look. "I hope you're not here on behalf of your family's university to urge me to change my beautiful realm back from glass."

"Not at all, your highness," Sera said. "It's a wonder to behold, and I thought it was quite unfair of the university to turn your beautiful glass statues back into people the last time we visited."

"Really?" Quentin looked surprised and a little pleased. "Well, it's nice to know someone in the Nayrlanda family has some taste. It's a shame my castle sorceress isn't here; I think she'd have liked to hear this. She's been taking care of some business for me and hasn't yet returned."

Wen wondered if Quentin had set his sorceress on other places besides Telsa. If so, he was very sorry for the people there, but he was rather grateful he and Sera didn't have to deal with the sorceress on top of Quentin.

"Prince Wenceslas and I were traveling through the area and I told him we simply *had* to stop to visit you and your shining castle. I was hoping perhaps you would still have some small collection of—*ahem,* glass statues that we might tour. Prince Wenceslas was ever so keen to see them."

Quentin looked at Wen, who tried his best to look extremely enthusiastic about the idea of seeing people who had been turned into glass, when all he felt was disgust toward a prince who would do such a thing.

"I would guess these are far more marvelous than the ones my father restored," Sera said, and that little push was all Quentin needed.

"You would guess right, my lady!" Quentin put out his arm, and Sera placed her fingers on the edge of his elbow, the smallest hold she could possibly have and still be touching him. "Allow me to give you the tour of my collection."

Quentin led them through several corridors and up numerous staircases, along another corridor and then up a winding staircase that led into a huge hall with a few doors leading off of it. The enormous hall was arranged with several dozen glass people. Men, women, a centaur, a unicorn, three faeries, a goblin, an ogre, and even two children. Their expressions ranged between cowering and fearful to wide-mouthed as though they'd been screaming. The two children were holding each other's hands and crouching on the ground.

"Whose children are those?" Sera's tone was tight, as though she was fighting for control of her emotions.

"I don't know. They wandered into my palace out of nowhere with some sob story about their father abandoning them in the woods. Boohoo, they couldn't find him and wah, wah, wah, some witch in a gingerbread house tried to eat them. Children are such a nuisance, don't you agree?"

"I'm actually quite fond of children," Sera said, even more strained.

"Well, everyone has some quirks," Quentin said dismissively. He motioned to a small statue—not quite a child, but when Wen got a closer look at her glass face, he realized she had to be very young. "And this young lady is the princess of Laudlin. Her father and I couldn't come to an arrangement to my satisfaction. I did promise to return her if he showed me that he could hold his allegiance to me for a year. He has eight more months to prove himself."

Wen's hands clenched into shaking fists. He wondered if he might get the jump on Quentin before Quentin could turn him into glass.

Sera affected an air of enthusiasm. "Ooh, do you have any other royals in your collection?"

"As a matter of fact, I do. Only one more, mind you—it wouldn't be wise to have too many royals, now would it? Otherwise word would get back to your meddling family."

"My family *is* quite good at meddling," Sera said.

"But I think I sufficiently pressed it upon the king of Laudlin how very many things could happen to his glass daughter should he tell anyone she's here." Quentin led Sera over to a figure of a bearded man whose frozen face was twisted into an angry expression. "And this is King Rodolph of Telsa. He is my most recent acquisition. I wish to marry his daughter, you see. I thought perhaps this would be a good incentive should my other plan not come to fruition—not that I expect it to fail, but it's good to have a back-up plan." He gently stroked the king's glass cheek. "Though it would be a shame to let him go."

Wen suppressed a shudder and Sera's fingers twitched

128

next to her club.

A wide grin on his face, Quentin turned so suddenly that Sera's hand was pulled from his elbow. He spread his arms to Wen and Sera. "You must be my guests for this evening. I insist. I'll have rooms prepared for you for tonight. Come. I'll show you the rest of my castle."

Quentin proceeded to show them everything he possibly could in his castle and grounds. There was the mirror room next to the hall of glass people—Wen was convinced the prince had this room so he could preen at himself; Quentin certainly flashed a lot of smiles at the mirrors. The mirrors were all different sizes and shapes; some hung on walls, others were freestanding and moveable, and Quentin adjusted several as he beamed at his reflection.

There were the gardens and a portrait hall—Quentin pointed at past relatives, but since the portraits were all glass, it was impossible to tell what the pictures actually looked like. At this point, Wen was convinced that Quentin was quite mad. Insane and arrogant were a dreadful combination in anyone, but in a powerful seventh son of a seventh son who was also royalty, it was a recipe for disaster and suffering.

After that, it was dinner, and Quentin insisted they eat with him. Wen could hardly choke down the food in his desire to knock the horrible prince into the next kingdom. Even the soldiers and servants seemed as wary and frightened of Quentin as the townsfolk.

By the time Wen and Sera were escorted to guest rooms, Wen's eyes ached from all the shiny, reflective surfaces. The glass bed frame had a soft mattress and warm blankets on it, and Wen gazed at those colors to ease his eyes a bit; he had half expected Quentin to have taken it into his head to turn those to glass, too.

Not that Wen would be sleeping in it. He and Sera had a lot of work to do and only five days until his birthday. They needed to be out of Hollin's End by morning.

His door cracked open. "It's me," Sera whispered.

"Come in."

She slid through the door with a surreptitious glance over her shoulder and then closed it quietly. She slumped against the wall and let out a huge rush of air. "He's out of his mind! And I thought he was out of his mind before all this. He's even worse now."

"I know."

"It took all my effort not to start screaming insults and hitting him with my club up there in that awful hall, but I didn't think I'd be able to get my club out before he could cast his glass spell on me."

"Listen, Sera, we can't just leave all of those people up there. Those children..."

"I know; it's dreadful what he's done to them. Those poor darlings."

"How did the people from Nayrlanda restore the glass people last time?"

"A restorative spell. In this case, we're actually lucky that Quentin's a seventh son of a seventh son, because he's not really using traditional magic. I mean—" Sera paused. "You know how I said that spells are supposed to come with an out?"

"Yes."

"Well, seventh sons of seventh sons are usually gifted with some incredibly powerful magical abilities that can circumvent some of the normal magic rules. Quentin didn't have to give these people an out—they could stay glass forever."

"But..." Wen said slowly. "Wouldn't that also mean there's not a specific thing you *have* to do to break the curse?"

"Yes, exactly. That's the upside to this. That's why a restorative spell will take care of it."

"This would be easier if I had some of those incredibly powerful magical abilities," Wen said.

"Honestly, I think you might be better off without them. You're not at all arrogant or mean or crazy like some *other* seventh sons of seventh sons." Sera bounced on her toes. "Are you ready to sneak back up to the hall with me?"

"Yes. The sooner we can fix those people, the sooner we can get out of here."

"I don't know what to do about Quentin. His room is undoubtedly guarded. I'm torn between going after him myself and waiting for Nayrlanda University to send a team of sorcerers and sorceresses."

130

"If you want to fight him tonight, I'll stand with you," Wen said. "It might be wisest to send for a team, though."

"Let's take it one step at a time. First, rescuing the people."

They made their way through the corridors, avoiding any soldiers they came across, until at last they climbed the winding staircase to the huge hall of glass prisoners. Burning torches on the walls of the hall cast an orange-red light over the sparkling people.

Wen looked around cautiously. "Why are the torches lit?"

"Maybe they're kept lit every night. Who knows? Quentin's mad, remember? He could like coming up here in the middle of the night, and maybe he doesn't like starting the fires." Sera moved quickly toward the figure of King Rodolph. "We need to move quickly." She pointed her club at the king and a rainbow came out of the end of it, hitting the glass and reflecting colorful beams of light all around the room.

"Pretty, but *no,*" Sera grumbled. She jabbed her club toward the statue again.

This time, it started to change. The top of the head turned into gray hair, and then the whole head and face became colorful, with skin and warm brown eyes, and next the shoulders and chest, like a wave of life running from head to toe, until King Rodolph stood flexing his fingers and looking around warily. He quickly took in the situation around him. "Who are you?" he asked Wen and Sera.

"Serafina Nayrlanda and Prince Wenceslas of Eirdane," Sera said hastily. "Your daughter sent us to look for you. Excuse us, please, your majesty, but there are a lot of other people I need to restore."

"Of course," the king said. "What can I do to help?"

"Just help me keep them calm when I wake them up. We don't want to draw any attention. The prince who did this to you is very close by." Sera moved to the two children and Wen followed her. It again took her two tries to do the restorative spell, and then both children came to life from head to toe.

Both looked around in confusion. "Where are we?" the little boy asked.

"I want Papa!" the little girl moaned. "Have you seen my papa?"

"No, but we'll help you sort this out later," Wen assured them. "Why don't you speak with this kind man?" He motioned to King Rodolph, who immediately wrapped an arm around each child and led them to the side of the hall.

"I'm going to do the ogre last," Sera muttered as she moved next to the goblin. "She'll probably be in a wretched mood and I don't want her smashing the others because she's so grumpy."

The princess of Laudlin was after the goblin. Once she was unfrozen, Wen could tell she wasn't any older than twelve or thirteen. Her dark curls shone in the torchlight and she burst into tears as soon as she realized she was free. She was so terrified of being turned into glass again that she panicked. Wen was certain her screams were going to bring Quentin.

"Shh, shh, it's all right!" Sera assured. "Here." She reached into the bag at her hip and pulled out the magic necklace she'd used to get through the gates in Nayrlanda. "If you wear this, it will keep anybody nearby from knowing you're here."

The princess got her words out between gasps of air. "It-it-it will keep that horrible prince from seeing me?"

"Yes, but no one here will be able to remember you. You'll be safe, but you'll be forgotten by anyone close by as long as you're wearing this, so it's very important that you take it off as soon as you're safe, do you understand?"

"Yes. Yes, I understand, I'll be careful, I promise," the princess said.

Sera slid the necklace over the princess's head, and then she and Wen looked at each other, uncertain why they were crouching on the floor when there were still people to restore.

It took Sera two or three tries each time to get the restorative spells functioning, and soon there were some toads, a fox, a ukulele, two rabbits, a bush, and a group of bats around the room as a result of the failed attempts of Sera's magic.

Halfway through, Sera was exhausted. Her shoulders drooped, her face was pale, and she moved with effort to the next glass person.

"Why don't you take a rest?" Wen murmured in her ear as she bent double and braced her hands on her knees.

"Might not...have time..." she wheezed, straightening and moving onward to the three faeries.

"Sera—"

She thrust out her club and a radish dropped to the ground. One of the rabbits nearby hopped over and sniffed at it. Sera gave another determined jab with her club and the faeries began to change. Wen caught Sera under the arms as her knees buckled. The rabbit, which had begun nibbling on the radish, was startled into hopping away.

Then Wen's blood ran cold when Quentin's furious, hysterical voice shrieked, *"What is the meaning of this?"*

15 – The Most Brilliant Sorceress

Wen supported Sera with one arm and turned to see the prince standing at the door, his eyes popping as he shoved his hands into his hair and stared around the hall. He looked absolutely insane. "My statues! My beautiful statues! YOU!" His crazed eyes landed on Wen and Sera. "What have you done?"

He held out his hands toward them, and Wen reacted instinctively, yanking Sera flat to the ground. A blue streak that looked almost like lightning shot over their heads, hit a statue, bounced off of it, and struck one of the women that Sera had restored. The woman turned instantly to glass.

"We have...to draw him away." Sera spoke between shallow breaths, still exhausted from all the magic she'd done.

Wen grabbed Sera and rolled them both over as another flash of blue hit the ground where they'd been lying. He eyed the door nearest them, the one that led into the room of mirrors. "Come on."

In one swift movement, he leapt to his feet, pulled Sera to hers, and raced with her to the door. "Over here, you ugly, conceited *prince!*" Wen shouted.

Quentin howled with rage. The force of the glass spells he sent at them cracked the doorway as Wen and Sera threw themselves through it. They ducked behind one of the freestanding mirrors, hiding from view of the door. Sera pressed a hand to her chest and struggled to breathe.

"Where are you? Show yourselves at once!" Quentin was in the room with them. His voice echoed off the walls, and his footsteps clanked on the glass floor, away from where Wen and Sera were hiding.

There came a long, piercing whistling noise that reverberated louder and louder around them. Wen froze, a thrill of foreboding racing down his spine.

"You won't be able to hide now!" Quentin screamed. "She's coming! She's coming! She's—"

His third "coming" was drowned out by a tremendous sound like a thousand plates crashing to the floor as the far side of the mirror room exploded in fragments of glass. Wen poked his head around the corner; there was a gaping, jagged hole in the outside wall. The dark night sky, twinkling with stars, was clearly visible, and then a monstrous head filled the hole and Wen's heart seemed to turn into glass.

It was a dragon. Not just *any* dragon: it was clear and shiny and...

"Glass," Sera whispered at Wen's shoulder. "A glass dragon."

"How is that possible?" Wen asked.

"I don't know. Maybe he turned a dragon into glass and then animated it with magic? Or maybe he found an existing glass dragon? It's *flying;* that's amazing!"

Sera shoved Wen out from behind the mirror and landed on top of him, and just in time: Quentin had snuck up on them and tried to blast them with his glass spell. Sera waved her club at him and a swarm of butterflies hit his eyes.

"Blast it!" Sera waved the club again, and Quentin fell flat on his face—except his feet were unmoving, stuck to the ground as though glued there.

The dragon spotted them—though how it could see with its eyes looking as glassy as the rest of it, Wen hadn't a clue—and roared its rage, but instead of breathing fire, the same sort of blue lightning Quentin was using came from its mouth.

Sera and Wen ducked across the room, dodging glass light beams thrown at them from Quentin, who was still frozen to the floor behind a wide mirror. They hid behind another mirror while the glass magic rebounded off of the walls and mirrors until it escaped out the broken wall.

"Quentin's stuck," Sera said. "We need to do something

about that dragon!"

"What do you bet it can turn things into glass, too?" Wen asked.

"I know some sorcerers have familiars, but this is like nothing I've ever seen!"

The dragon continued to smash at the wall, seemingly desperate to fit into the room. Some of the mirrors closest to it had been crushed into the ground. Glass fragments flew through the air and clinked against the mirror Wen and Sera were hiding behind.

"I can't slay a glass dragon," Wen said. "My sword won't do anything!"

"Wenceslas! That magic! The magic you told me the faeries gave you for saving them from that newt—use it, and then you can't turn into glass and the dragon can't kill you. You'll have an hour and you can bring down Quentin and figure out how to—"

The mirror they were hiding behind was slammed out of the way. The glass dragon's head was mere meters from them. It had managed to clamber into the hall of mirrors and its body took up a fourth of the room. Glass fragments from the walls spilled off it as it shook its wings. Wen covered his face with his hands, but shards of glass sliced his hands and arms.

Sera leapt up onto the dragon's face, scrambling for a hold on the slippery surface, as Wen ducked between its legs. He was almost crushed and jumped to the side of the dragon just in time. He got a quick glimpse of Quentin yelling something, though over all the noise of crunching glass as the dragon stepped on the broken pieces, Wen couldn't hear his words.

The dragon roared more magic. The magic went straight toward Quentin, who used the wide mirror as a shield to keep from getting hit with it.

The dragon shook its head forcefully and Sera got one leg over the ridges around its face. When the dragon realized that wasn't going to shake Sera loose, it turned and smashed its head against part of the wall it had not broken. Sera's back slammed into the wall and her head bounced back and hit it. Blood blossomed on the glass, and the dragon swung its head again. This time, Sera's hold slipped,

136

and she fell off the dragon and straight out the broken wall. She grabbed onto the edge of the hole, dangling from the opening high, high above the ground.

"Sera!" Wen leapt across the broken glass, and his knees hit the ground as he seized her wrist. Sera cried out in pain—her hands and arms were cut and bloodied, and there were likely glass shards in her skin. The thick leather of Wen's trousers was the only thing that protected his knees from the glass beneath him. "Just hold on, I'll get you up."

They were so high up in the castle that it was dizzying. The cottages below, gleaming in the moonlight, looked miniscule. Sera's wrist, slick with blood, was slipping from his grasp.

"My club! I dropped my club!"

"Sera!" Wen struggled to keep a grip on her, panic clawing at him as she slipped a little farther.

There was no response; Sera stared down, where her club tumbled end over end to the streets below.

"Serafina!"

Her eyes snapped up to his, then widened. *"Duck!"* she screamed, and he flattened himself to the ground just as the dragon's tail tried to take off his head. His shirt was *not* made of protective material, and the broken glass under him cut into his skin, like getting jabbed in the chest with a hundred sewing pins. His eyes watered and blurred, and with a great heave, he pulled Sera up and back into the room with him, dragging her to the side as the dragon roared more of its blue lightning at them. The lightning went straight out the hole in the wall.

Sera clutched Wen's arm. She was spattered with blood, and her clothes and skin were cut all over the place. "I can't help you without my club!"

They moved behind the length of mirrors on one side and ran toward the fore of the room, away from the dragon. Every movement sent surges of pain through Wen's torso, every motion dug the glass in his skin a little deeper. He was sure that, like with the burning monster blood back in Telsa, his heart was pumping so hard and fast he probably wasn't feeling the full impact of the injuries yet. "You don't need a club, Sera!"

137

"Yes, I do!" she yelled. "I can't do magic without it! I can't do magic right the first time even when I do have it!"

"But you do it right in the end! You *are* brilliant. You are the smartest, cleverest person I have ever known, and you are a sorceress, and it's never been about a club. It's *you*. It's always, always been you."

The dragon whirled around and smashed the mirrors they were passing with its tail, and they were thrown against the wall. The dragon stomped through the mirrors it had knocked over and its mouth came down, not blowing glass sparks, but opening its jaws wide and snapping down at Sera. In that split second before its teeth closed over her, Wen smacked his hand into Sera's chest and shouted, "Niamin!"

The dragon's mouth closed over Sera's head, but instead of biting it off, the teeth couldn't shut. The dragon shook its jaws and Sera's body was flung from side to side like some horrible ragdoll, and when it still couldn't behead her, it opened its mouth and she flew into the middle of the room, landing with a crash on a pile of broken glass.

Sera jumped up and yelled, "Wenceslas, I told you to use that on yourself!"

"Right, so you could get your head bitten off." Wen clambered to his feet as the confused, angry dragon turned to eye him glassily again. "You take care of Quentin."

Quentin was still frozen near the door, and he seemed to think Sera made a great target standing there in the middle of the room. He held out his palms toward her as she said, "I still don't know *how* without my club! His feet might be stuck, but he can still fight if I get close—oh! OH!" She looked down at herself as the glass magic washed over her without any effect whatsoever.

Quentin's face twisted into an ugly expression. "How? *How is that possible?* You should be glass! You should—"

He was again drowned out by the dragon's roar. Wen took a page out of Sera's book and leapt onto the dragon's head. He pulled himself up over the top of it, leaving streaks of blood from his many cuts, and slid down onto its back. He caught himself on one of its ridges. The dragon snapped and snarled and tried to turn its neck to see him, but Wen's position on its back made it impossible for it to get at him.

"Wenceslas!" Sera called. "Keep the dragon distracted!"

"I'm trying!" It was all he could do to stay on the bucking, raging creature. He glimpsed Sera at the front of the room, running around and moving mirrors, tilting them at certain angles. Then she picked up a large, broken piece of mirror and held it in front of her.

"Hey, Quentin! You horrible, evil, disgusting excuse for a prince!"

Quentin screamed and screamed and threw blue magic at Sera from around his mirror. Wen watched in amazement from the writhing dragon as the magic reflected off the mirror Sera held and hit another mirror. It ricocheted off of several more mirrors that Sera had positioned, then the ceiling, and struck the top of Quentin's head.

His screaming stopped abruptly as he turned into glass. In that moment, the dragon shuddered and shook violently, and then collapsed onto the ground, becoming as still as a statue.

Wen remained where he was on the back of the dragon. "Is it...dead?"

Sera walked over and poked it in the eye. "It's frozen, I think. I'd guess its life must have been tied to Quentin's. I'd run a diagnostic spell to be sure, but my club's somewhere way, way down on the ground."

Wen slid off of the dragon, swearing inwardly the whole way down to keep from shouting out in pain. He crunched across the glass toward Sera. "You got him to turn himself into glass."

She waved a hand. "I just calculated the angles of the mirrors. I was afraid if I didn't hit him from above, he'd realize what I was doing and block the magic with the mirror next to him. And I was worried the dragon would smash it all before I finished."

"You were brilliant. You *are* brilliant."

"What you said—I never thought that maybe I've misinterpreted the seer's prediction all this time. My parents were so sure I had to be fantastic at sorcery, but maybe...could it be that the seer meant I would be brilliant *and* a sorceress? Even...even if I'm not really a good sorceress?"

"It sure seems that way to me."

139

Sera beamed at him. "I'd hug you right now, but that would probably hurt you a lot."

Wen was sure it would. Razor sharp pain shot through his upper body with every movement. "Wouldn't it hurt you?"

Sera moved her arms around. "I'm all better. The glass is gone and my cuts are healed—so is the lump on my head. That faerie magic fixed up everything that was already hurting me." Her eyes swept over him worriedly. "Come on. Let's take care of you. Don't move."

Starting with his arm, Sera gently daubed ointment on him. "The ointment will dissolve the glass, I think," she murmured. "It's supposed to get rid of anything foreign in the skin before it heals an open wound."

Cool relief crept over Wen's arm as Sera continued to apply the ointment, then his other arm, his face, neck, back and chest. He was grateful when she was done and the only trace of his wounds was the blood left behind.

"All right." Sera tucked the ointment away. "Now I'll get my club and finish restoring those poor people. I also need to send a message to Nayrlanda University to update them on the situation and let them know they can get out here to finish up—there's no way I can restore all of the buildings and fields. And then we need to get King Rodolph back to Jessalin."

Some of Wen's elation drained away. "Right."

He and Sera picked their way through the ruined mirror room, past the glass figure that had been Quentin, and back into the hall of glass people.

"King Rodolph?" Wen called. "It's safe!"

A few heads poked out of a room farther along the hall, and then King Rodolph stepped out. His eyes went round with shock at the sight of them. "Oh, my! You're terribly hurt!"

"We're fine, really. We just look awful," Sera said.

"What happened to Quentin?" King Rodolph asked.

"Turned to glass by his own spell," Wen said. "Thanks to her."

"I'll need my club before I can do any more restoring," Sera said. "It fell out the wall of the mirror room and it's somewhere on the ground."

140

"I'll see to it that it's found," King Rodolph assured.

The princess of Laudlin appeared in front of them, holding Sera's magic necklace, and Wen suddenly remembered that she had been there all along.

"Thank you," the princess whispered, and she hugged both Wen and Sera and burst into more tears. "Thank you, thank you." She didn't seem to mind that she was getting their blood on her dress. "Here's your necklace back."

Sera tucked it away and held the princess's face in her hands. "We'll make sure you get back to your father, all right?"

"Thank you."

"I believe we may have found the true king of Hollin's End and the prince heirs," King Rodolph said. "Apparently Quentin didn't banish his brothers very far at all." He motioned to Wen and Sera and disappeared back into the room he'd exited earlier.

Wen and Sera went after him. The room they walked into was small and narrow in comparison to the hall and the mirror room. There were seven coffins, three on either side and one alone in the middle at the end. Each coffin held a glass figure in it. Wen guessed that the six on the sides of the room were Quentin's brothers and the one in the middle was his father.

Sera immediately stiffened. "Glass coffins."

Wen knew what was on her mind, because he was thinking it, too. "The fairy godmother giftcurse is supposed to give me until my birthday."

Sera still looked wary.

King Rodolph left the room and soon came back with one of Quentin's soldiers, who held Sera's club.

"Word's spread around the castle that you defeated King—that is, Prince Quentin," the soldier said. "And on behalf of all of us, *thank you*. Thank you. You've freed us all." He placed the club gently in her arms.

Sera smiled at him and turned back toward the glass coffins. "Let's see about fixing the king and princes." She tried to lift the glass off the coffin of the first prince. It wouldn't budge.

"It looks like it's sealed." Wen ran his fingers along the base and bent down to look at it more closely. "There are no seams." He drew his sword and gently tapped the glass with the hilt. The coffin shattered and Wen jumped back; he was more worried about getting sliced up again than he was about his giftcurse. "We just need to brush all the glass off the prince before you wake him up, or he might get cut."

Sera ripped off a part of her very torn skirt, wrapped it around and around her hand, and carefully used it as a sort of broom to sweep the shards off the prince.

Using this process of breaking the coffin and sweeping off the glass, they soon had the princes and the king uncovered, and then Sera began restoring them.

Wen stood at the edge of the room, watching her bring them back to life and making sure she didn't get so tired from the magic that she collapsed. Bloodied, her hair half torn out of her twist, her dress ripped and missing some of its pearls and jewels, she was the most beautiful girl he had ever seen.

His boot crunched on one of the shards from the shattered coffins. He stared down at all the glass for a long moment. The words the drunken fairy godmother had spoken over him, which his mother had told him so many times over the years, revolved around in his head.

"Wenceslas shall be a great hero. He shall rescue a princess from her enchantment and marry her by his seventeenth birthday, and failing this, he shall prick his finger on a glass coffin and he shall die."

Even though she had amended this to a sleeping enchantment, did she really have any idea what she had condemned him to? Years of searching, years of trying to find a princess to marry so he could have his life back... until Sera had come along and convinced him he didn't have to settle.

At this point, though, marrying *any* princess was going to be settling.

Sera's reminder rose up in his memory. *"There's always a second option. You just have to look for it."*

Wen bent to the ground and gingerly picked up one of the coffin shards. He pulled out a handkerchief, wrapped it around the glass, and tucked it carefully into his pocket.

16 – True Love's Kiss

It was an hour from the arrival of Wen's seventeenth birthday when the thorn-surrounded castle in Telsa came into view. He'd traveled speedily with Sera, King Rodolph, and the soldiers Rodolph had had with him when they'd all been turned into glass. The others who had been restored were taking care of themselves, or, in the case of the children, being taken care of by others who had agreed to help them.

Once King Rodolph had heard the whole story about Wen and Sera rescuing his daughter from the sleeping enchantment, Wen's giftcurse, and his agreement with Jessalin, he had considered Wen gravely before saying, "If my daughter accepted you, she must have seen your worth. Her judgment has never yet failed. And I saw your courage in rescuing us. You have my blessing to proceed with marriage, if that is Jessalin's wish."

Wen stared at the approaching castle, his resolve growing with every kilometer. He knew exactly what he was going to do.

"I must see my daughter," Rodolph said. "And we will arrange a wedding as quickly as possible, Wenceslas."

Wen brought Bay to a halt. "I have something to do first," he said. "And maybe last," he murmured under his breath so that no one could hear him.

"Very well." Rodolph and his guard continued on toward Telsa.

Sera brought Butter around to face Wen. "Are you all right?"

"Are *you?* You've been getting quieter and quieter the

closer we get to Telsa."

Sera shifted on Butter. "I guess I've just been thinking about what I'm going to do once you get married. I think I may be ready to go face my family. Tell them that even if they believe that seer meant I would be good at sorcery, I've come to think otherwise, and I'll be *me* and not what they expect me to be."

He smiled. Then his smile faded as he glanced up at the half moon. He swung down off Bay and whispered, "Wait here, Bay."

As if Bay understood how important this was, he whickered softly and nudged Wen with his nose. Wen rubbed his nose affectionately, his throat suddenly a bit tight. "You're a great friend, Bay," he said softly. He gave Bay one final pat, then walked over to Sera and held up his arms. "Come walk with me?"

"Wenceslas, you have less than an hour until your birthday. You're probably safe until at least then, possibly even on your birthday, but that's not guaranteed. Your fairy godmother said you had to marry a princess by your seventeenth birthday—that could mean by the end of it, or it could mean by the start of it—"

"I know." He kept his arms up.

Sera frowned at him, but she finally slid off of Butter into his arms, and he set her on the ground. She was dressed simply again, in trousers and a soft blue shirt. Her helmet and breastplate were both attached to Butter. "Well, at least if you are too late for marriage to fulfill your giftcurse and you do prick your finger, you're already here where Jessalin can get to you quickly."

"Mm," he said noncommittally.

"I mean, you found your true love, and that was really the point of all of this anyway, don't you think?"

Wen smiled at her.

He didn't have a particular destination in mind; he wanted to pass the last hour of his sixteenth year walking with Sera and staying away from the town, and so he took them in a wide berth around it. Wen and Sera shared stories of their childhood with each other, and then moved on to talking about their nieces and nephews. Sera kept glancing upward at the sky, undoubtedly ticking off minutes

144

until she had to watch out for glass coffins.

Finally, Sera turned and faced him. "It's past midnight now."

"Yes."

"Happy birthday."

He smiled a little. "It's funny. This birthday has dominated my entire life, and now that it's here...well, it's amazing how things can change with a little perspective."

Sera wrapped her arms around herself as a chill breeze cut across them. "What are we doing out here, Wenceslas, really? Jessalin is probably wondering where you are, and...and..."

She trailed off and pressed her lips together.

"And?" he prodded.

"Nothing. Never mind. Let's go, Wenceslas."

She had only taken two steps toward the town when he said, "Sera," and she turned back.

He held up the handkerchief he'd just pulled from his pocket and slowly unwrapped it. She moved back toward him as he held aloft the glass shard wrapped in the handkerchief. "I brought it back from Hollin's End. It's from one of the coffins we broke."

"It—*what?* Wenceslas, *why* would you—"

"Because I'm done. You made me believe I didn't have to settle for a princess I didn't want to be with, and guess what? I haven't found that princess. Do you know what I found? I found *you,* Serafina Nayrlanda."

Sera's breath hitched.

"When you asked me where I most wanted to be, I wasn't entirely honest. Yes, I'd like to be home, but my home will be empty now if you're not there. I know you don't feel the same way about me," he said hurriedly. "You were so upset with me when I was under the influence of the love potion, and you want me to marry Princess Jessalin. You've been helping me all along so I could marry someone else, but when you asked me if I'd be miserable marrying her, you didn't let me finish what I was trying to say. I was going to tell you I didn't know if miserable was the right word—it was more like agonizing. Because it's not Jessalin that I love, it's *you.* And I would rather spend eternity in an enchanted sleep than a lifetime without you."

He pressed his finger against the sharp shard of glass, and blackness immediately engulfed him. He vaguely felt himself falling and heard Sera saying his name, and then sleep held him fast in its grip.

The next thing he knew, he was waking up to Sera's face above his. He blinked. "Sera?" The night sky looked exactly the same as it had when he'd fallen asleep, with the same half moon hanging in the sky. "How long was I asleep?"

"Oh, for about five seconds. You idiot!" Sera cupped his face in her hands and pressed a kiss to his lips. *Another* kiss; it had to have been she who had kissed him awake.

A wonderful, glorious feeling like lightning in his veins jolted through him. Wen sat up, wrapped his arms around her, and tilted his head to better reach her. It was a million times better than when he'd kissed her under the love potion.

"You went and pricked your finger without even giving me a chance to answer you!" Sera said when they finally separated. "That wasn't fair."

"I didn't want you to try to talk me out of it."

"Tch. If you had let me have a turn," she said pointedly, "I'd have told you that the day we met Jessalin, when you reminded me that you were still going to help me find something to run toward, I knew I'd already found it. It was *you*. And when I kept looking at my magic compass, I saw that no matter where I had it, it only ever pointed toward you. And I was upset with the love potion because it made me realize there was no way you could love me unless you were under the influence of a potion."

"That's not true, I—"

"Shut up, I'm making an exasperated sorceress speech. I just wanted you to be safe, and Princess Jessalin seemed perfect for you. She's everything I said and more. She's... she's tall and has pretty hair and she doesn't look like she's only twelve years old!" Sera waved down at herself, a slight blush blossoming on her cheeks.

"Oh, Sera." He pulled her close again and covered her mouth with his. She made a happy little noise and wrapped her arms around him with such force that she knocked him back onto the ground.

146

Eventually, half dizzy with sheer giddiness, they helped each other to their feet.

"I suppose we should tell King Rodolph and Princess Jessalin that there isn't to be a wedding after all, before they get too busy with the planning," Wen said.

"And then what?" Sera asked.

"And then…home. I can go home. My giftcurse has been fulfilled." He beamed at her. "Come with me. Please."

"Oh, my darling Wenceslas. Always. Except—there is that trip to my family that I should make first."

"I'll come with you."

"Father will be ever so pleased," she said very dryly.

They went back toward the town hand in hand, Sera skipping the whole way.

***

It was late evening when Wen and Sera arrived again at the Nayrlanda estate. Lights shone through all of the windows, and more hovered all along the garden path up to the front door. Sera had sent word that she would be paying a visit to her family on this night, and between the lights and the two guards waiting at the gate, it was obvious they were expecting her.

"Lady Nayrlanda," one of the guards said, bowing slightly. "Allow us to escort you to the house." His eyes flickered briefly over Sera's shirt and trousers, but he didn't comment.

"He's coming, too." Sera held tightly to Wen's arm. Her voice was light, but the grip she had on Wen told him how very nervous she was.

The guards eyed Wen but didn't argue with Sera. They simply bowed again and led Wen and Sera up the path.

"They're afraid I'm going to escape," Sera whispered. "My family."

He pressed his hand over the one she had clinging to his arm. "You're going to get through this."

"You say that now. You haven't ever been in a room with all of them."

"I suppose I'll have to get used to it."

"Algernon will like you," she hastened to assure. "He and

I poke at each other and he can be irritating sometimes, but he was always the most supportive of me." She squeezed his arm. "Oh, what am I doing?"

"You know exactly what you're doing." Wen stopped on the middle of the garden path, and the guards paused to wait for them. "You are the most determined, confident person I have ever known. You are *you,* not them, and who you are is more than your name, or your family, or the words of a seer, or anything else."

Sera let out a deep breath. "I know. I know." She rolled her shoulders. "All right. Let's do this."

They resumed their walk to the door. The guards escorted them inside and through the house to some large double doors. One of the guards knocked on a door, opened it, and poked his head inside.

"Excuse me, Lord Nayrlanda, Lady Nayrlanda," the guard said, "your daughter has arrived." He glanced at Wen. "With a guest." He stepped aside, revealing a large sitting room with a blazing fire, where Sera's family was gathered: her parents, two brothers, two sisters, and a man who had not been in the family portrait, whom Wen guessed to be Delphina's husband. Her children weren't present; perhaps they were already asleep.

Sera stepped inside, still holding Wen's arm, and for several seconds, her family stared at them in silence.

Then Sera's mother clapped her hands to her mouth, an expression of horror dawning on her face. "Oh, darling! Your clothes!"

At the same moment, Sera's younger sister, Elisabette, cried, "Sera!" She flung herself on Sera and squeezed tightly.

"Hello, Elisabette darling," Sera murmured.

"Serafina, what are you wearing?" This came from Sera's elder sister, Delphina. She looked as scandalized as her mother. "And with a young man present?"

"And what have you done to your hair?" her mother asked despairingly. "You have—you have *bangs.*"

"Yes, I have bangs, Mother," Sera said in exasperation.

"Serafina, how could you do this to us?" Lord Nayrlanda demanded.

"What, my hair? It was quite easy; I took a pair of

scissors and—"

"Enough of your cheek, young lady!" Sera's father pointed a finger at her. "I am talking about you running away from Sorceress Lillian and not sending any word for three months! What is the matter with you?"

"Is it true you turned her roof into a volcano?" Sera's younger brother Reginald asked in interest.

"Reginald," Lady Nayrlanda reproved.

"*You* switched my strengthening potion for a love potion." Sera jabbed her finger toward Reginald. "I'll turn you into a volcano if you don't watch it."

"Serafina," her father said warningly.

"Father, I left Sorceress Lillian because she had all the compassion of a dragon and her breath always smelled of garlic," Sera said.

"Your father and I worked very hard to get you an apprenticeship with Sorceress Lillian," Lady Nayrlanda said sternly. "You are being *rude,* very rude indeed."

"Your mother is quite right. You don't leave your apprenticeship simply because you don't like the way you are being taught or the way your teacher's breath smells!" her father said, while her mother nodded agreement. "How do you ever expect to be a proper sorceress if you cannot have the basic decency to treat your instructor with respect? We didn't raise you to be a barbarian!"

Sera's elder brother, Algernon, brushed past his family to reach Sera. He crushed her in a hug, which was the only reason she finally relinquished her hold on Wen.

"It's good to see you safe," he murmured to her. When he released her, he rolled his eyes backward in the direction of the rest of their family, and Sera gave him a grateful smile. He turned to Wen and held out a hand. "Algernon."

Wen shook his hand firmly. "Wen."

"He's a prince of Eirdane," Sera said.

Everyone's attention immediately shifted to Wen.

"A prince? Serafina!" Delphina exclaimed. "What did you do to him!?"

"What? I didn't do—" Sera began, but she was cut off.

"Oh, Serafina," her father groaned. "Is he under an enchantment?" He leaned closer to Wen and peered at him carefully.

Wen jumped when something brushed his leg. The two-headed cat wound around his feet.

"I did not enchant him!" Sera said indignantly. "All right, well, I put a couple of enchantments on him at different times, but nothing long-lasting! In fact, I unenchanted him."

Wen bowed politely to her family. "She did," he agreed. "She broke a fairy godmother spell on me that had afflicted me my whole life."

Her family's gaze shifted back to Sera.

"Is this true?" her father demanded, his eyes narrowed doubtfully. "You broke a fairy godmother enchantment? How?"

A smile spread across Sera's face. "It was an enchantment that could only be broken by true love's kiss."

"*What?*"

"True love's kiss!?"

"With a prince? Oh, Serafina!"

"Ooooh, are you going to marry him?"

"Elisabette, what sort of a question is that? He's a *prince,* Sera wouldn't—"

"Oh, I would," Sera spoke over her mother. Her family fell silent again, and Sera looked at Wen, who nodded at her encouragingly. "Not now, but sometime. We'll do it in our time, in our way."

"Serafina, you have studies to attend!" Lord Nayrlanda's eyes blazed and he towered commandingly over Sera. "Your sorceress's training is—"

"Finished," Sera interrupted. "At least the way you want me to do it, Father." She shook her head and took a step back beside Wen. "I'm done trying to live up to everyone else's expectations. Wenceslas helped me to see. I'm brilliant. I'm a brilliant person." She said that without any hint of arrogance, simply stating a fact. "And I'm not very good at sorcery, but I'm still a sorceress. I *am* a brilliant sorceress."

Her family went quite still, except for Algernon, who crossed his arms, smiled dazzlingly at Sera, and gave her the tiniest of nods.

"I'm a Nayrlanda, but I'm not any of you. I don't want to be. So I'm done with what everyone expects of me. I'm done running away and thinking I'll never be good enough for you." Sera looked her father squarely in the eyes. "I came here to tell you goodbye. I finally found something to run toward. And once I reached it, I found someone to run with me. I wouldn't trade that for all the magic in the world."

Epilogue – Ever After

Their wedding took place several years later. The ceremony was held on the bluff overlooking Authian Bay, outside Wen's family's castle, and it had some of the most unusual guests any wedding had ever seen.

King Rodolph and Princess Jessalin were there, and Princess Rapunzel and her husband, and some of the former frog princes. Prince Humphrey was with Esme, the princess who had kissed them out of their frog prince spell. Her eleven sisters were all there as well, having been rescued from their dancing enchantment by the minstrel Sera and Wen had met on the road. The minstrel, almost unrecognizable from the wretched man he had been that day, was beaming on the arm of his dancing princess. Prince Charming of Whares was showing his arm muscles to several of the giggling, blushing sisters. Sera's childhood friend Penelope was beside them. Rumpel Stiltskin was avoiding sitting anywhere near any of the babies in attendance. Beside him was Beeswax the dwarf.

There were centaurs and faeries, unicorns and pixies, and two ogres, which the castle servants were keeping a very wary and close eye on. So many faces, stretching a good distance back, come from far and wide to celebrate this day with Wen and Sera. There were crowds of people from towns and kingdoms that Wen and Sera had rescued or visited, both on their initial journey together and afterward, as they had, from time to time, left Wen's castle to go adventuring.

"It's nice to be able to do this because I want to and not because I have to," Wen had said on more than one occasion,

152

and Sera always countered that by adding, "And it's nice to have a home to come back to afterward."

His home on the sea had become as much hers over the past years. His mum had been over the moon when Wen had brought Sera back to the castle, and his mum had immediately set to work making one area of the castle just Sera's, including giving her one of the towers where she could have a telescope to see the stars. And Sera shared Wen's love of the ocean and the breeze that came off of it and the wide, sweeping paddocks where Bay and Butter could run together.

Sera's parents were in attendance with all of her siblings, nieces, and nephews. Elisabette, who was quite taken with Wen, waved exuberantly at him from her seat beside her parents. He smiled and waved back while Sera's parents looked on rather disapprovingly. Algernon caught his eye and winked hugely at him.

Wen's father was grouped together with Wen's brothers and their families, all talking animatedly. His mother stood in front of Wen, squeezing his hands and saying something, but he was so distracted he only realized she was talking when she said, "And then his head fell off and rolled right into the bay."

"What?" Wen asked, startled.

His mum's green eyes twinkled. "I wondered if you were listening. How are you, dearest?"

"I think facing dragons is less nerve-wracking than this."

His mum laughed. "Then you're doing beautifully." She gave his hands a final squeeze. "I'm going to go sit down now. The wedding's about to start. You're going to be fine. Trust me."

She lifted her skirts and went down the stairs to join the rest of Wen's family. Then the wood elves from Helane began playing their music, and the crowd before Wen parted, and there was Sera. Her wedding dress was pale blue and far plainer than her mother had liked, her bangs were as short and wispy as ever, and she hadn't grown a centimeter since he'd met her.

A wide, dazed grin split across his face. She had her club in one hand and her helmet in the other. The crowd was whispering about that, and he even thought he heard

Sera's mother groan. His eyes were fixed solely on her; his stomach danced as though a million butterflies had erupted in it.

Wen's sense of time and everything else around him seemed skewed and unimportant as Sera came to a stop in front of him. The castle sorcerer who was officiating their wedding looked between them, and Sera cleared her throat.

"I wanted to bring these"—she lifted the club and helmet—"to show that I'm giving everything I have to this. To you. To us." She swallowed. "This"—she placed the club in his hand—"to show that even though I've never been a very good sorceress, you've believed in me anyway. Even if you still cringe when I point it at you," she added, and the audience laughed.

"And this"—she put the helmet in his other hand—"to show that even though I've got armor, I trust you to watch my back more than I trust that."

Wen held the club and helmet close to his chest, and she whispered, "I expect those back later."

He choked back a laugh, whispered, "I know," and set them gently next to his feet.

He unbelted his sword and handed it to her. "We'll fight our battles together, and I'll always look out for you the same way you look after me." He reached into his breast pocket and pulled out his handkerchief with the glass shard from the coffin. He set it in her hand. "Without you, I would be asleep. Maybe not physically asleep, but always, in my heart."

Sera's eyes sparkled. She pressed up on tiptoes and tugged Wen down to kiss him.

The sorcerer officiating cleared his throat. Sera waved at him dismissively, still kissing Wen, and finally dropped off her tiptoes and released Wen. "All right," she said graciously to the sorcerer. "You may proceed now."

More titters from the audience.

The rest of the ceremony flew by. They made promises to each other, and the sorcerer wound a glowing thread around their wrists and joined hands, proclaiming Wen and Sera husband and wife.

Cheers exploded from the crowd. Wen lifted Sera off her feet and spun her around, kissing her, until he felt dizzy and Sera was laughing against his mouth. The world was spinning when he set her down. He picked up her club and helmet and handed them back to her. She returned his sword and said, "I'm going to hold on to the coffin shard."

"To all of our friends and family, thank you for coming to celebrate with us today!" Wen called.

Sera lifted her club and pointed it up above the crowd. Light shone from it and a long, thick viper burst from the end of it, right into the middle of the crowd. It reared up, hissing, and Sera said, "Oops."

Algernon snapped his fingers and the viper vanished.

Sera waved at him in thanks, then pointed her club upward again. Many in the crowd cringed, but this time, swirling stars and sparklers burst out of her club, exploding overhead in showers of color and drifting down around the wedding guests. There were many "oohs" and "ahhs" and some of the children ran to try to catch the light as they would snow.

Wen offered his arm to Sera, who took it, beaming, as she set her helmet on top her head. "And then they lived happily ever after?" he suggested.

"How about, 'and then they lived adventuring and loving ever after?'"

"I like that one."

"So do I. Oh, blasted bat wings, the ogres and the pixies are getting into it."

Wen followed Sera through the crowd toward the fighting wedding guests. "And then they lived breaking up fights between ogres and pixies ever after."

Sera flashed him a grin as she dodged a group of seven dwarves in attendance. "That works, too."

Acknowledgments

Through a long, convoluted, complicated three-year writing journey, this book went from YA romance to MG friendship and then back to the YA romance I had originally intended it to be. I have a deep love for Wen and Sera; they helped me learn a lot about myself and what I wanted out of my writing.

A lot of people were involved in what this book was, changed into, became, and ultimately is now. Thank you to everyone who had input, believed in the story, encouraged me.

Thanks to my husband, Ryke, who has ridden one heck of a roller coaster with me while I sorted through a million different things in my mind and in pursuit of my writing. Thank you for being there to hold me up and talk me through my hard places.

Thanks to my kids who encouraged me with their laughter and enthusiasm.

Thanks to all of my beta readers on this book: Ryke, Quinny, the Crew, Melanie, Emily, Emma, Faith, Barbara, Cheryl, Brenda, Steven, Jess, Shanna, Jeana, Donna, and Megan.

Special thanks to Natalie Lakosil, for the opportunity and chances you took on me, and for giving me the encouragement I needed to find what I really wanted for this book.

About the Author

Laura Josephsen is an editor and a long-time writer. She's a fan of Korean dramas, anime, manga, video games, sci-fi shows, fantasy stories, socks, and crocheting. She enjoys coffee quite a lot. She lives near the Texas coast with her awesome husband, imaginative children, many cats, and numerous hermit crabs.

Made in United States
North Haven, CT
28 September 2023

42103602R00104